Demimonde
The Other Story

Marla J. Selvidge

ISBN:978-0-9895808-1-6

DEDICATION

For Thomas C. Hemling, Ph.D. who has and always
will be the great love of my life.
His humor, confidence, and care sustain me!

CONTENTS

AN ANCIENT CLEANSING

It was in the thirty-third year of the gracious Emperor Caius Octavius Caepias Augustus that a woman and a man-child were brought into the world by two Roman subjects of high distinction. The father was brother to the Emperor, senator and world-renowned general. The mother was said to be a mistress-queen belonging to the house of Ptolemy of Egypt. Their love for each other ended the night Augustus burned them alive before the Coliseum doors for their treasonous crime of passion. It was reported that the male child was sacrificed to the Gods as a peace offering between Egypt and Rome. The woman-child was taken into the house of the Emperor and raised as his own. He named her Magdala, which meant "adulterer."

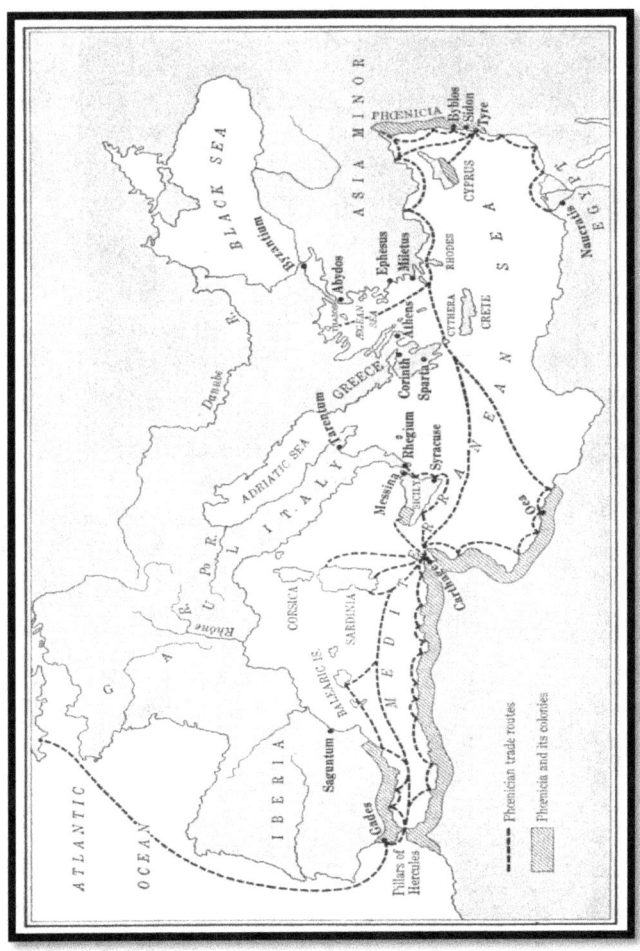

Prologue: Ephesus

C.E. 72

"Ephesus was a city full of strangers these days. In the old days no
one was a stranger."

Long ago the first worshippers of the thousand-breasted Artemis,
patron fertility Goddess of the city, called themselves Amazons. These
women took no husbands. Yet once every year, usually in the spring, like a
herd of thirsty cattle, they made their way down from the mountains to the
streets of Ephesus. For that night and that night only, they would seduce
all healthy, young men they could find. For some strange reason, men
always gave into their advances. Some young men claimed they were forced
to have sex with several of the women at the same time. Whatever the true
story, each year the Amazons conquered Ephesus. They took nothing back
with them except the hopes of bearing a child. Before the end of the year,
abandoned male babies, often dead or dying, were found on doorsteps
throughout the city. Amazons kept only the female babies.

In spite of the sexual raids in the spring, Ephesus had flourished under
a strong Roman infrastructure that fostered peace. There was time to enjoy
life. Since the time of the ancients, cultic prostitution had been a central
part of its splendid culture. Daily, both priests and priestesses stood or sat
on the steps of the temple waiting anxiously to bring pleasure to the next
lonely devotee

Times were changing. The massive stone structures of the city like its
never-ending spring fed water below its streets had always been invincible.
Now amidst the turmoil of an influx of refugees from the wars in the East,
less support from the wealthy aristocrats within the Roman guard, and a
weakened priesthood, Ephesus was crumbling. She was dying from within.

Some said that Zeus had put a curse on the city. He was angry with
the Amazons because they had kept all the female babies for themselves.
The Amazons had stolen the heart of the Ephesus. The discarded souls
and deaths of the male children were bringing vengeance on the city.

With tears streaming down her golden-covered breasts, Artemis no
longer hailed every passing ship inviting them to visit her temple and city.
Sadly she sat near the edge of the water and watched her playground for the
rich become a dangerous infested swamp.

CHAPTER ONE
EPHESUS

"In Ephesus the nights are dark and women who are alone do not stay that way for very long."

Magdala's heart burned for her lover, John. She had spent the last year of her life and most of her great fortune scouring the coasts of the Mediterranean in search of both John and her beloved, Phoebe. Imprisoned during the devastating siege of Judea by the Romans under Titus, Magdala had lost contact with her loved ones who had been living in the north, in Galilee. While the devastation was not as great in the north, people had been burned or uprooted from their homes and taken as slaves by the Romans. Some escaped into the hills. After thousands of faces and almost as many letters Magdala's persistence was rewarded. Only a few days ago a private courier had delivered a hand-scratched message from John.

Magdala could barely read the note, she was very ill. Some said that she had only days, perhaps weeks, to live. The fevers had destroyed much of her lovely body. Hygeia had implored her to make her way to a northern climate where the cool breezes would provide relief from her disease. She sought refuge in the snow-covered mountains near Bithynia. In Thyatira, several hundred miles north of Ephesus, Magdala and her personal healer, Hygeia, lived a cloistered but restless time away from the hot suns of the desert surrounding Ephesus for a few months. Magdala longed for John, he was on her mind day and night. But as the months passed, she convinced herself that both he and her daughter were either taken as slaves or killed during the wars. With disbelief she read the note.

"My dearest Magdala, At last I have found you. It seems like an eternity since we were together. I am in Ephesus at the Asclepioi House. Come to me. I have heard that Phoebe is also alive. She is in Rome and will arrive in a few days. I would come to you but I have been arrested by the Romans and they will not allow me to leave the city. With all my love, I anxiously await your arrival. Waiting, John

Magdala and Hygeia packed their trunks and began the long trek to Ephesus. They traveled for days over rivers and rugged land that was almost inaccessible. Weary from the journey and the mountain terrain, they sought refuge for the night in a forgotten sanctuary. Entering the abandoned temple, they discovered blood stained murals, broken pots, and crushed furniture. "Magdala, I think we should leave. We have desecrated the sacred space of the dead who are buried here," advised Hygeia. "Hygeia, it is so cold outside, don't you think that we will be safer in here than out on the open road? It looks like no one has been here in a very long time," argued Magdala. "Magdala, I can hear voices, so many voices," cried Hygeia.

In spite of their feelings about the temple, both of them decided to make camp in its ruins. They would be safe for another night. As they arranged their things and sat down beside a warm fire set by Hygeia, Magdala began to dream. Her thoughts took her back to Galilee, to the hills surrounding Capernaum. She would never forget the day that she found John and Lysander, the magician.

Looking across the fire at Magdala, Hygeia wondered about her far-away look. "What are you thinking about?" "I was just thinking about the day I found John and Lysander." Hygeia said, "Who did you say?" "Lysander!" "Magdala, I can't believe it. All these years we have been together and you never mentioned him." "Did you know him also, Hygeia?" "Yes, it was a very long, long time ago. He was very young." "Magdala, where did you meet him?" And Magdala began to tell the story.

It began in Capernaum. I had been staying with a Jewish woman while visiting the baths, the healing centers in Galilee. Everyone I visited for help told me the same thing, I was dying. I had contracted a fatal fever and there was no cure. Then I met Lysander.

"Please don't go near this wonder-worker, Lysander, you don't know what might happen to you," cried Alda, the old woman who had been taking care of me. She had chosen the life of a widow and made her living by housing people who came to the baths. Alda had spent the past forty years living alone and taking very sick people to the baths. Alda cried again, "Magdala, you know the ancient laws. If you have a fever and are in your monthly courses, you must hide yourself. You should not be out in the streets by yourself. You might touch someone. You are disobeying the Divine."

"Leave me alone, Alda. I have tried everything. I have been sick for so long. The bleeding has gone on for years and no one will talk with me any longer. They say I am in Niddah all of the time. They say that my disease is dangerous to everyone and it is fatal. The physicians cannot help me. They won't even touch me, but they take my money all the same. This Lysander is my last chance. Besides I am not a Hebrew, I don't believe in all of your laws. I am going to ask him for help."

Alda retorted, "So what if you do ask him? Do you think he is going to talk, let alone, help a woman with Fularia? They say he has Jewish blood. Why would he risk his life for you? I wouldn't even discuss your woman problem in public, let alone let the whole world know about it. If those people out there knew that you had that dreaded disease, they would probably tear you to pieces. You are out of your mind, I would not risk it." "Alda, I have spent so much money on physicians and no one has been able to cure me. What do I have to lose," pleaded Magdala, "You could lose your life," stared Alda. "Alda, I am so weak, the fevers have taken all of my strength. I know that I only have a little time left."

Alda tried to reason with Magdala, "Those novices of his will stop you. Why they would not even let Lysander hold some of the babies the other day. I heard that they told all of the children to go home. The novices want all of his attention. "Alda, I have to try it. I have heard so many stories about him. I know that if I could only talk with him that he would do something for me. Oh, look, there is a crowd gathering over there by the lake. Let's go and see if they are surrounding Lysander."

Lysander was attempting to walk up the hill from the Sea of Galilee. People from the town had rushed out to see him, and they were pushing up against him. Some were shoving others out of the way. Many had camped along the southeast side of the lake for days waiting for Lysander. There were rumors that he had the power to heal and that he would give you food.

On the way into town, people lined the streets with their arms outstretched. Some were barely clothed while others were clean and dressed in expensive cloth with jewels. There were a few Roman soldiers. Some of the diseased, crippled, and grotesque thrust their bodies and mouths at Lysander. They wanted him. Not everyone could get to him so they kept pushing and pushing. To be near him might make their dreams come true.

Many believed that their suffering, pain, or illness would retract if they touched him. These people had no income and survived on the garbage and throwaways of others. The streets were the only home they had ever known. They stayed for only a few days in a town and then would walk to another one. Like a chorus they chanted, "Have mercy on me." Please look this way and help out this woman who has no children." "If you would only touch me, I know my dried up leg or arm would work." "Help us. Heal us. Care for us. We are so alone in this life. We need you. You have the magic. You care for people. We have heard of you. You have the touch of the Almighty. You can change our lives. You can bring life to dead eyes, we have heard. Make us alive again. Make us happy. Make us rich."

The commotion was so thick with dust that you could scarcely see that the cloud coming toward Lysander, toward Capernaum, was human. Lysander was somewhere ahead of the cloud. People were trampled within the frantic mob. Their crushed bodies were ignored by the seekers. People in search of hope have no time or care for others. They want only something for themselves. This was a chance of a lifetime. Women screeched and babies screamed under the pressure of surging bodies scrambling toward Lysander.

"There he is Magdala, I see him," shouted Alda. Stories about Lysander were wrong. People had said that he was a tall, dark-skinned man with long curly hair. Contrarily, Lysander was not any taller than the smallest person in the crowd. His long golden blonde hair fell over slightly rounded shoulders. One of his eyes was black and the other was blue. On one arm he bore a huge black scar and the other was black. He had no facial hair and wore a long-green garment.

Magdala ran ahead to the synagogue. Could this be the man whom everyone is talking about? He looked so ordinary, maybe even a little rough. Was this the man that stood up in a public meeting and challenged the people to take care of others, who claimed that the ancient words had been fulfilled in him, that he had been sent by the Star God? Some said that he was going to be a liberator, a freedom fighter for all of the people. More than once, as they say, he tamed an angry crowd with just a word or cold stare.

From the top of the steps Magdala could see that Lysander looked like a Macedonian not a Hebrew. Some said that his mother was from Asia Minor, a Jewess who had been born a Gentile and converted to Judaism. She claimed royal blood and that her child came from the Divine. Others said that he was a bastard who had no father and that his mother was a woman who sold her body at the local well.

Lysander slowly made his way up the hill towards the temple. He stopped and helped all that he could along the way. His healing touch did not work for everyone. Some regained their strength but others died in their attempt to touch him. Some walked away with nothing and more desperate than they had ever been. They had lost their last hope.

Magdala stared at Lysander's simply clad body. The anguish of so many helpless and needy people was etched into deep lines under his eyes and beside his mouth. There was only one of him but so many of them. His power could not reach them all. With small and tender hands he touched a pock-marked and bleeding leper and a hopelessly dying child, too limp to walk. Magdala had heard that he was a laborer, yet his body was slight and he seemed weak, not strong from working in the fields. Flanking Lysander were several young men who tried to protect him. The tallest had dark flowing curls with a very long-well-kept beard. He looked like a sorcerer. Compared to Lysander he was calloused. He commanded the rest of the men.

Climbing down from the steps of the synagogue Magdala made her way toward Lysander. Every step as she pushed her way through the crowd seemed to take her breath away. Her pounding heart felt as if it was going to explode. Finally within a few feet of Lysander, she thrust herself toward him. She was suffocating, "If only I could touch him, I know I would feel better. His touch will help me."

With arms high as she pushed she suddenly fell to the ground, but it was an open space. She had even crashed through the men surrounding Lysander, his novices. Lunging toward him, she grabbed at him and caught the edge of an old coat. Without being provoked, Lysander, turned around and searched the mass of human flesh. Magdala lay beneath the crowd who were trampling her.

Lysander exclaimed. "Who touched me? Who touched me? Where is she?" The crowd stopped silently waiting for an answer. No one understood his outburst. Again he shouted at the top of his lungs, "Who touched me?" Magdala knew that his screams were her death notice. Fingers around her began to point toward her. She was lying face down in the mud. Lysander's novices did not understand. Everyone on the street wanted to touch him. They were mystified at his reaction because they had watched many hundreds; perhaps thousands of people touch him.

Magdala was caught. At the exact instant that she touched the edge of the coat of Lysander, she felt a surge of energy that she had never experienced. It was like a blast of lightning that hit her from her feet and came right through the top of her head. Was this the disease of the Gods? She felt stronger, was she really going to live? She thought, "If I tell him, he might take away this feeling. He might kill me?" So, she got up and dusted off her clothing and walked straight towards this mysterious man. "I did it! I touched you. I think I am cured after all these years. You did it, Lysander, you brought me back." Lysander was puzzled. "Woman, what is your name? "Magdala, Sir, " she sighed. He looked straight at her and said, "This has never happened. I am not sure what you have done? I felt a loss of energy. I did not will it. I did not want to let it go. You took it from me. You brought the energy to you, I did not."

Thunderous roars broke out in the crowd. They began to chant. Great is Lysander! Great is Lysander! Great is Lysander! Lysander offered his hand and walked with Magdala. It did not matter that the Jews had laws against such touching in public. He had already broken the rule to never speak with a woman in public. Almost instantaneously, the young men around Lysander rushed toward him. Like dogs on a fox hunt they surrounded her and hurled angry insults, spat upon, and pushed Magdala. Her presence was an insult. She was a woman, only a woman, and a woman who had a fatal womanly disease that everyone feared.

With terror in her eyes, Magdala stepped back towards Lysander. A tall dark-skinned man reached out for her and pulled her away from the young men. Within seconds they were out of sight of the moving throng headed up the hill together. That dark-skinned man was called, John, son of Zebedee who had lately moved East from Ephesus to Galilee. She was safe. Never did she dream that someday she would find love within and for him.

Magdala's thoughts drifted back to Hygeia who was staring into the fire. So much had happened to both of them since those days so long ago. Magdala stretched out on the floor and curled upon into a blanket. Hygeia stared up into the altar of the temple. She could not believe that Magdala also had known Lysander. Without another word, they drifted off into a troubled sleep.

Morning broke and with it the travelers headed for the city. City life was exhilarating after months of quiet in the mountains. As they approached Ephesus, on top of the great pavement, they could see the ocean. Walking toward the water the old rutted street narrowed where people were setting up their food carts. A heavy haze hung over the mud brick shanties lining each side of the pavement like listless children with no place to go.

Ephesus had been the best city in the world. Now its marbled buildings were tarnished with forgotten care. Everyone who was anyone in the Empire had visited Ephesus. Its marvelous beaches and interesting shops attracted visitors from all over the globe. Now the faces of people seemed drab and lifeless. Where were the Senators, the soldiers, and the foreign dignitaries that made Ephesus their second home? As they walked closer to the shore hawkers would not leave them alone. They even came up and put their hands on their arms and tried to open their bags to find money or food. Merchants were now beggars too!

They turned around and walked back toward the city. A thick dark haze surrounded the buildings. The closer they got, the more difficult it was to breathe. Fires were smoldering here and there as they searched for the street that led to the temple. After about three hours of following streets that went nowhere, they found the Asclepioi residence. Standing before its huge ornately carved doors they were horrified to see blood dripping down the cracks. Deeply imbedded in the door was a gold-handled knife. Magdala pulled on it, but it would not budge. They beat on the doors so long that a crowd was forming outside the gate. Someone wanted to keep the world outside the gates.

Suddenly there was a scuffle toward the back of the wall around the house. Magdala and Hygeia followed the crowd to a small opening. They crawled through the opening to the garden. Hygeia screamed. "What is it? What is the matter?," quipped Magdala. Magdala turned around and looked toward the top of the house. There was something hanging in the tree near the cold spring. The object was swinging. It was a man. "Oh, my God, Hygeia, it is John," cried Magdala hysterically. John's clothing was in shreds. He had scrapes and dirt all over him. He had been drug through the muddy streets.

The onlookers began to shout and push each other. Within seconds the street was jammed with screaming bodies thrusting rocks at each other, a daily occurrence. Magdala's head began to swoon. "We must find a place to hide," whispered Hygeia as she grabbed Magdala's arm.

She took Magdala by the hand and headed for a shop owned by a friend of Hygeia's, Lydia of Philippi. Suddenly, out of the mob a cloaked shadow surged toward Hygeia and violently threw her to the ground. Magdala tried to help her up to her feet but a leg was broken. "Don't move me. Find an Asclepioi Priest," beckoned Hygeia.

Magdala had no idea of where to find an Asclepioi. Angry faces were not about to help her with anything. She did not understand what was going on in the city. The military guard began moving in to squelch the disturbance and there was no mercy for the people in the streets. They were whipped and kicked brutally when the guard moved down the pavement with their carts. Magdala ran down an alley off the main pavement and found herself, luckily, standing in front of the Asclepioi temple. Not far behind the shadowy figure was dogging her every step.

Up the steps, Magdala banged on the door, " I need help. Please help me. Help me!" Running around the back of the temple, she found a servant working in the priest's cottage. "Help me, can you help me? Where is the priest? I need help. My healer has been hurt. She is lying in the street. Please help me" "Madame, " explained the servant, "I am the only one here. But, come, I will try to help you."

Magdala led the servant back to the street where Hygeia had fallen. She was gone. A crowd of motionless people stood on the spot where she had been. Magdala looked into the empty faces and screamed, "Where is she? I have to help her. What have you done with her? Where is she? Out of nowhere a huge figure wearing the golden image of fire broke into the crowd and headed toward Magdala once again.

CHAPTER TWO
THE SACRED FIRE
6 C.E.

"Sometimes we have no choice."

Life could never be easy for a child who had no parents. Magdala came into the world as a problem and that history followed her everywhere she went. She survived only because Augustus wished it, no more or no less. Her earliest recollection was at the Temple of Fire in Rome. To sanctify the deeds of her parents, Augustus declared that she should be dedicated as a Vestal Virgin. At the age of three, and only by the decree of Augustus, Magdala was ordained a Vestal Virgin.

One of the greatest honors in the Empire was to be chosen to become a Vestal. The most exclusive and affluent families under the strong arm of Rome lobbied for the sacred positions. Only a handful was chosen each year. Women would take a sacred vow of celibacy for thirty years. One of their most important duties was to keep the sacred fire of Rome burning. Most saw the temple of fire as a symbol of the state of Rome. If the fire went out then the nation would die.

In return for their chastity and solemn pledge to serve the state, they were given access to the most privileged information. They did not have to bear and raise children nor did they have to run a house for a husband or family. They were present at all official functions of the state and acted as couriers for the Emperor and other international officials. Together they guarded the Treasury of the entire Empire.

Vestals were treated like queens. They were carried through the streets on golden chairs held high above the crowds. Many worshipped them, and most respected them. Because of their highly visible and sensitive position in the state, any infraction of their vows could result in capital punishment. It was rumored that in the past some of the vestals had broken their vows of celibacy. For their infractions the high priest had them beaten severely and walled up alive in a stone tomb.

Today Magdala was to take the sacred vows. She was dressed in white and wore a wreath of ivy around her dark brown hair. She stood with seven other maidens who seemed to be very proud of their selection to serve Vesta and the state. Magdala did not understand what was happening to her. Augustus had adopted her after the execution of her parents. She was told that she had been an abandoned child. Now Augustus was abandoning her also. The ceremony was full of festivities. People were dancing, singing, and swirling together in the streets. Magdala dutifully and obediently stood with the others and greeted the devotees and heads of state.

When the time finally came to take the vows, a rotund man in a black robe with a golden flame embroidered on his chest appeared before the crowd on the pavement in front of the temple. His voice rang out over all the noise in the streets, "Zeus, our God and hope for the future, and Vesta our Queen, look down upon us today. We dedicate the minds, hearts, and bodies of these young women to you." One by one each young maiden walked toward the huge fire in a cauldron beside the temple steps. The rotund priest dipped an iron into the seething molten liquid and held up a stamp that bore the mark of the Vestal Virgins.

The maidens, so beautiful and innocent with their fair skin and soft features, seemed out of place, strange. The mob anxiously awaited the final step in the festival. One hesitant maiden stepped forward. The priest asked her a few questions and she responded. She raised her hands above her chest and closed her eyes. Bellowing, the priest reached for the heavens, "Isis, Zeus, Vesta, Hera, and all watch this child for she shall be yours for the next thirty years." And with that cry he plunged the red-hot iron stamp upon the left cheek of the child. She screamed with pain, fainted, and was carried away by onlookers. One after another each maiden came before the priest and each received the mark of her new vocation.

Finally Magdala was called. She walked forward to the giant, dark man. Beside him sat Augustus and his family. Magdala thought, "This must be what it is like to stand before all the Gods." Slowly she climbed the steps. They were so large that she almost had to crawl from one step to another. When she reached the top of the steps, the crowd gasped.

Hundreds of people began whispering, "Take the child away, she is too young. Who allows this child to take an oath? Why she is not even twelve years old. Take her away, she is too young."

With a large hammer, the priest hit the side of the steaming cauldron. The sounds echoed in the mountains and returned. The chanting stopped. "By the wish of Caesar Augustus this child will become a virgin for Rome. Silence, Silence, Silence." Turning to Magdala, the Priest spoke," Magdala, do you promise to keep the sacred fire of Rome constantly burning for the next thirty years?" Magdala stood silent. "Do you promise complete allegiance to the worship of Vesta and the desires of the State?" Magdala stood silent. "Will you remain a Virgin for thirty years?" Magdala stood silent. "Do you promise to represent the state and watch over the receipts and monies kept in the sacred Treasury at the temple for the next thirty years? Magdala stood silent. "Do you now give your life to the Gods and hope that through this act of yours you might live with them some day?" Magdala stood silent. "Spread your arms up to the Gods and hope that they you have the strength to keep all of your vows." Magdala stood silent and would not move.

Two men in ritual clothing came toward her little body and forcefully lifted her arms. The stinging of the metal sizzled on her cheek. In extreme pain she fell down at the feet of the dark priest. As long as she could remember anything at all, she would remember this day. Every time she looked in a mirror the emblem of the sacred fire would stare back at her.

14 C.E. Rome and Its New Ruler

"No one ever left Rome without acquiring a taste for power."

Mars, the God of war, reigned in Rome. Near the gate of Carmenta the Romans built a temple to honor their war God. Many important affairs of state were held in the foyer of this magnificent shrine. The priests of Mars were chosen from amongst the finest and most brutal gladiators on earth. In front of the temple stood a huge metal column. In the event of war, one of the priests would take a spear and strike it. The noise could be heard throughout the villages.

Seeds for this great city, say the ancients, were planted with greed wrapped in violence. Mars, a handsome and virile God cunningly raped a Vestal by the name of Rhea. Out of this unearthly union were born two sons Romulus and Remus who were abandoned in a basket along a river. A she-wolf found them and lovingly nursed them until they were old enough to live on their own. Decades later Romulus killed his only living relative, Remus, over a land dispute.

Romulus founded the city of Rome in an empty field where he had buried his brother. His city became a haven for pirates and outlaws. Realizing that a city does not grow without women, Romulus sent henchmen into the neighboring cities and outlying countries with the sole purpose of stealing women. These unfortunate captives were forced to bear children for the new city.

Now millennia later, during the days of Augustus, all who visited Rome vowed to return. It was magnificent. Her majestic structures, rambling forum, and impressive coliseum filled people with everything they needed. The administration was strict to the point of brutality. The games were thrilling and the food was delicious. Even the slaves had a good life. Nowhere in the entire world could anyone find a better place to live. Augustus' Rome was the finest and most peaceful city in the Empire.

But in the days of Tiberius, Rome reverted back to the times of Romulus. It became a haven for the power-hungry and greedy. Under the hand of an irrational Emperor human life was expendable. To disagree with any decision of the state could mean immediate torture and death. Tiberius who inherited the throne on the death of Augustus was moody and did not like living in Rome. Most of his life was spent on the island of Capri. Rumors had it that he would maim and torture his friends for sport. Justice was now in the hands of lawless men and women who followed the despicable example of Romulus.

Life at the temple was not unlike living with the Emperor. He had demanded that she be treated well. After all she was much too young to participate in any of the state events or carry letters from one official to another. Occasionally she would be carried in a covered chair through the streets to sit before Augustus at the opening ceremonies of a game or of the Senate. She was an ornament of the Emperor and a symbol to him of the chastity that he wished his brother would have had so many years ago. So Magdala grew and learned to live the life of a Virgin dedicated to the State.

The duties of the Vestal Virgins were numerous. Some were ambassadors to other countries. Some were keepers of the Treasury or the Sacred Fire. Magdala was a novice to all the vocations and would eventually spend ten years learning each one. One night during Magdala's fifth year of service, she heard a loud scream coming from the sacred hearth area. Climbing out of bed she witnessed several gladiators carrying two Vestals and their richly garbed suitors into the streets below. All of them were chained to the chariots and drug over the pavement. The next day their heads were displayed in the marketplace as a warning to all who would break the vow of a Vestal.

Magdala left her room only a couple of times over the next few days. The voices and huge men that stood at the temple doors frightened her. Early on the third morning after the killings, the High Priest entered the temple during breakfast and explained why the two Vestals were murdered. On a random inspection of the temple, two of the Praetorian guards had discovered that the Vestals were entertaining men. The women were so enthralled that they had forgotten about the Sacred Fire. It died in the night some time.

A hush settled over the women. Since the arrest of the two Vestals no one had been allowed into the sacred area. Someone asked, "What will happen. Will we have to rekindle the Sacred Fire?" The High Priest, a tear rolling down his check, said, "We will have to sanctify the entire temple and pray that the Gods will forgive us." The Roman Empire has been compromised. It has no strength without the Sacred Fire. "How will we sanctify the entire temple? " asked a Vestal. "We will have to make the temple ready. We must purge it. It is made of stone so most of the structure will survive. Come, let's go to the Sacred Hall."

All of the Vestals followed the priest except Magdala. She had forgotten her sandals and quietly slipped away from the group. When returned Magdala returned to the banquet hall where they had been eating breakfast, she found it empty. She sat down at the table and waited patiently for someone to return. Suddenly the temple shook. It was like thunder.

Unknown to Magdala, the High Priest had taken all of the Vestals into the inner chamber of the temple. On his command the entrance doors were barred and shut. He gave the order, "Burn them." The guards protested, "What will the Gods do to us if we murder the Vestals?" "Pray that what we do here today is acceptable to the Gods. If it is not, then all of Rome will fall and you will no longer have to worry about your Gods," argued the High Priest.

Understanding the wisdom of the High Priest's arguments, the guards changed their minds and proceeded to pour oil over the top of the massive doors onto the women. "What is going on here," they complained. In the next second fire enveloped the Vestals and almost took the lives of the guards, who failed to realize that the fire would follow the streams of oil they were pouring. Weeping, the High Priest stood before the temple and proclaimed, "The Sacred Fire of Rome lives again. Accept this offering and forgive us for our great neglect."

Meanwhile, Magdala heard the screams and saw the smoke from the sacred chambers. She instinctively ran toward the cries of the Vestals pleading, "Open the doors!" Magdala could hear them kicking and scratching at the bolts that held the doors tightly shut and nailed together. With all the might of an eight-year-old Magdala tugged at the doors. It was no use. Her arms began to burn. The doors were immoveable. Falling to the floor, Magdala wanted to die too. She did not want to live without her sisters, her family.

Almost suffocating, when she fell to the floor where she dislodged a slab of slate covering a forgotten entrance to the temple. She scrambled through the ancient passageway. The dirt gave way under her feet and she began falling and sliding down a shaft. Finally she hit solid ground where she fainted. Waking up, she managed to stand up in the dark lonely tunnel The opening was actually an old aqueduct used by the builders of the temple to bring water to the sacred area while it was being erected. She walked for hours. Tiny animals swirled and crawled upon her feet and legs. Stench of rotting meat sickened Magdala. Where was she? Finally she saw a small light that seemed bigger and bigger as she walked. It was a hole to the outside. Exhausted she lay on the grass outside the hole and slept for two days.

"Wake up. Wake up, child. What are you doing in this field? Magdala could not speak. She tried to hide the mark of the Vestals. "Wake up child. Where are your parents? What are you doing here," said the kindly old farmer by the name of Philip. He was on his way to the market when he spotted Magdala lying on the ground. He was dressed in clean, plain clothes wearing a long white beard and sporting peering eyes. On his head was a funny little covering and strings of fabric hung outside a vest-like shirt. His hair was tied in a knot at the back of his head. Around his neck hung a silver star. "Child. Who are you? From where did you come? What are you doing out in the field?"

Magdala's clothing was filthy with burns in various places and torn by the rocks when she fell to the aqueduct. "Where are we?," she asked. "We are about a half hour outside of Rome. Are you going to Rome, little girl," asked the man. Magdala did not answer. "May I walk with you Sir?" "Better than that. Can you get up? Here, come over to my cart and you can ride on my vegetables." From where they stood you could see the gigantic walls of the great city. "How did I get so far outside the city?" thought Magdala. In the distance sounds of horses echoed. A military tribune and his attendances galloped by pushing the old man and his cart out of the way. As the old man tried to move it, it turned over spilling the sacks on top of Magdala. "Are you okay under there?" Magdala answered, "Yes, just get the cart off my legs. What happened? Philip did not know exactly. "One of the Emperor's soldiers seemed to be out of control. They were probably a special envoy from another country." While they were picking up the cargo, another galloped by them. Philip yelled, "What is going on?" "The Emperor is dead! Caesar Augustus is dead," he heard faintly.

Some say that after a leisurely vacation on Capri, Augustus lay down one evening and never woke up again. His death shocked the world. The God of the Roman Empire was dead. Tiberius Claudius Nero would soon reign as the new monarch in this ancient city. His brutality would touch the lives of every soul.

Weary, Magdala and Philip looked at each other. With that announcement about Augustus, Magdala's future died. She had no home, no parents, and now no Emperor. The city looked more like a dungeon than a home for a child who had no place to go. Together they headed toward Rome. Philip wondered about the little girl whose hands were dirty and burned but not calloused like his daughters. "What do they call you little girl?" "My name is Magdala." "And my name is Philip son of Abraham. Where shall I drop you when we make it to the city? "Coyly, Magdala answered, "Oh, I will tell you when we get there." But she had no place to go.

The walls are huge. You could race chariots on them. When they finally reached them, the main gate was barred. Centurions blocked the huge stone road. "May we pass," asked Philip. "The gates are closed until morning. All the people are in mourning because of the death of Augustus." Philip pleaded, "I must get my vegetables to the merchants before they spoil. May I pass so that I can deliver my goods?" "Sir," retorted the guard," the gates are closed. It is an official decree of the Senate. The market is closed. No one will open their shops today."

Philip backed up his donkey and cart and moved to the other side of the road. It was August but it seemed cold. Rain was coming. Other travelers had built a fire and were keeping themselves warm. Philip asked, "May we share your fire?" A very tall light-skinned man stepped forward. "You don't belong here. Find somewhere else to sleep. We don't like people of your kind around here. Go away and leave us alone." Magdala did not understand this harsh treatment toward someone who had been so kind to her. Philip did seem different from the other farmers. His long beard and colorful vest accentuated his odd eyes. But his manner always spoke of tenderness and care, not of mistrust, violence, or hatred like the others who were stranded.

Philip wandered off down the stone-lined road with his bags of fruit and vegetables. Magdala followed. A few feet off the road, he spread a blanket and fixed supper for Magdala and himself. Magdala was ravenous. She ate until she fell asleep. Philip wrapped her in his only blanket and placed her safely under the cart. He stretched out near his donkey.

Within a few minutes Magdala cried fitfully and shook. She sat up quickly and hit her head on the bottom of the cart. Philip ran over to her and took her in his arms and rocked her like a baby until she fell asleep. He thought, "Sleep my child. Morning will be here soon and we will find your family. The demons will not bother you tonight." So Magdala slept in the arms of Philip. She knew nothing about this old man but she had nowhere else to go. Little did she know that she would have a home with Philip for many years to come.

CHAPTER THREE
CHUSA AND THE FUTURE
C.E. 24

"A night in Rome could be your last."

"**N**o, no don't take him away. He has done nothing wrong. Let him go," Joanna pleaded. "Leave my father alone. You bastards. You mongers. He is innocent." The fraying ropes cut deep into Philip's ankles as the guards pulled him through the marketplace in front of the Forum down the hill. Philip had been delivering his vegetables as usual when a group of merchants ganged up on him. They began shouting, "Hey, Jew boy go home. We don't need your food here." "If it wasn't for your kind, we would be rich!" "Hey, are you a spy? Are you going to start a revolution here too?" "Take your vegetables away from here and to back to where you belong, you porcus-eater!"

The shopkeepers were losing money because shipments from the East had been delayed. Some Jewish revolutionaries had begun fighting with the Romans over land-rights and taxes. The war was getting so bad that many of the Roman offices had been shut down. Consequently supplies were not being sent through the usually efficient Roman import system. The ships were still tied up in the harbor. Many seamen were either being detained or were part of the uprising. Everyone was being watched and searched.

Three months without goods to sell had made most of the merchants nervous. Someone had to pay for their losses. Philip was a likely target. Discontented and without much to do, the shopkeepers jumped Philip as he made his rounds. Within seconds the entire marketplace was rioting. "Halt there," shouted a Centurion. "Halt or I will send you to the gladiators. What is this?"

The Centurion and guards took their spears and began forcing the merchants away from Philip. Philip lay on the ground in a pool of blood. His daughters ran to help him. In spite of his injuries, the guards placed ropes on his neck, hands, and ankles. Looking at the shopkeepers, they yelled, "What has this man done to you? He looks like a peasant." One merchant chimed back, "He's a spy, a Revolutionary! He won't worship our new Emperor as God."

The Centurion turned to a barely conscious Philip and asked if the charges were correct? Do you worship another God? Philip would not answer. "Man, what is the name of your God?" "Yahweh," said Philip. "Are you a spy," said the Centurion. "A spy? A spy for what or whom? I am a Hebrew, a Jew." That last answer was enough for the Centurion to find him guilty as charged. "How many standing here would give drachma to watch this spy die?" Several came forward with coins in their hands. When the Centurion's helmet was full, he said, "Let's do it!" One of the guards hitched Philip to the back of a horse drawn chariot and began dragging him down the street toward the cliff."

In a few moments Philip would be murdered. He would be thrown down the hill into the Tiber River. He would follow the path of many innocent Jews and others who fell victim to the whims of guards under the rule of Sejanus. These days in Rome, with Tiberius almost always on holiday, Lucius Sejanus ruled when he was gone. Both the innocent and guilty suffered under his rule. Only people with assets or something of value could escape his jurisdiction. Philip had neither.

Magdala and Philip's four daughters fought through the mob trying to catch up to the guards. They wanted to save him, but how? Lately it had become a daily event in the marketplace when the guards would murder an innocent person. The bloodthirsty crowds enjoyed the sport. Joanna, the eldest and most beautiful of Philip's daughters, grabbed the Centurion's horn and began to blow it. "Stop it! I have something of value to trade for the life of my father." The Centurion stopped, "Will it be worth more than I have collected?" "I would hope so, " said Joanna.

Magdala could not believe Joanna's words. They had nothing of value with them. Maybe it was a ploy to buy some time? Philip did own a parcel of land that he had inherited from his parents? The land was never to be sold. Joanna continued, "How much would you pay for a young virgin?" The Centurion and guards laughed and spit on her. "How do we know you are a virgin, big girl?" Magdala rushed toward the men but Joanna's sisters kept her back. "Joanna, are you out of your mind?" cried one sister. "What good would it do to sell yourself? How do we know that they would free papa anyway?" Joanna retorted back, "We have to do something." Joanna proceeded. "How much would you pay for a good slave? How much would you pay for a woman slave that could do the work of a man? How much am I worth? I am worth at least twice as much as any of your slaves. Someone shouted, "Hey big girl, can you read and write?" "Of course, I have been educated by my father. I write in Latin, Greek, and Aramaic."

Philip awoke from his semi-unconscious state. He was too weak to fight the ropes. The shopkeepers had broken several bones. He managed a faint cry, "No, Joanna, no don't do this. Let me die. I am not worth your life. Do not trade your life for mine. Joanna ignored her father's pleadings. The Centurion looked at the uneasy crowd around the woman. "Who wants to purchase her? The proceeds will go to the State. Let the bidding begin."

Magdala began to cry; she would probably never see Joanna again. Philip looked as if he would not survive. She had no power and no way to change the situation. She was helpless, again. When the bidding began, Magdala's mind was taken back to another time, to another day when she felt utterly helpless, the day that Augustus died.

Augustus was dead. The trumpets blew and the doors to the city finally opened. Black flags draped city walls and houses. Posters flanked blank walls; "Today is a day of mourning for Caesar Augustus. All recreation and commerce is banned in the city. " Philip sank into the wagon. One more day and his cargo would be rotten. He was carrying an entire harvest. The money was going to get them through the winter storms. What could he do? "Magdala, what am I going to do? I have to sell these today or they will ruin." Magdala thought. "Why not sell them outside the city. The edict is only for sales inside the city walls."

Philip turned the wagon around and went back to the crossroads near the Appian Way, the main road entering the city. There he set up a display of his vegetables, but no one bought anything. A few stopped and fondled some of his squash, but as soon as they saw him, they left. Some mumbled, "Porcus, grass eater, peasant!" "Magdala, this is not working. I am doomed," Philip mumbled to Magdala. "Philip, let's see if the people will buy the vegetables from me? Go hide behind the rocks." Magdala was right. Traveling people stopped in droves to buy the goods. Some would ask, "Little girl, where are your parents? Are you alone?" But Magdala did not answer. Soon all of the cargo was sold and Magdala proudly presented a large bag of money to Philip. He was stunned. Philip offered to give

Magdala part of the money but she refused. It was getting late and Philip knew that he had to find Magdala's relatives soon. "Where shall I take you?"

Magdala had no place to go. She thought it was not safe for her to be anywhere near the city. But she did not know that Augustus' will was read publicly that very morning near where she was selling vegetables? Tiberius was to be crowned Emperor. Magdala and all of Augustus' family were to divide the estate equally. Since Magdala was a Vestal, a special trust was set up of over a million drachmas that were designed to take care of her for the rest of her life. Everyone who heard the will believed that Magdala had been sentenced to death by the High Priest with the rest of the Vestals earlier in the week.

Philip could not believe such a well-educated and bright young girl had no place to go. "Have you run away from home? If you have, I am sure that your parents love you. Tell me where you live and I will take you there." Magdala asserted, "I told you, I have no home, and there is no place where I will be welcomed." Philip had no choice. He was not going to abandon her. He harnessed the donkey and headed south with Magdala by his side. "Come stay with us for a while, I have four daughters who I think you will love."

Magdala never told Philip about her background because she thought that she was an outlaw. She managed to avoid questions about the sign of the Vestal on her cheek; it was a good luck birthmark. And later, she learned how to apply coloring to hide the mark. Generally she wore her hair in a way that covered the sign. When she left Rome, few knew had ever seen the sign of the Vestals. Every day she feared that someone would discover that she was a Vestal and then she would be executed too. Little did she know that the high priest had murdered the Virgins in direct opposition to the Emperor's orders? So Magdala hid herself among Philip's family in the south of Rome for fifteen years.

The donkey tripped along the huge stone road while Philip sang a Hebrew chant, "Baruch etai eluhenu...." Magdala wanted to know the name of the tune and what it meant. Philip explained, " I am singing, blessed is our God." I am a Jew and this is how we begin our prayers. Magada asked, "What is a Jew?" Philip explained that he was different from other Romans. He worshipped one God and they worshipped many, although they claimed to worship only the Emperor. He ate different foods and celebrated different holidays. While he was not a very strict Jew, he did enjoy his heritage and tried his best to keep all the ancient laws and ritual practices.

In all of her studies at the temple, Magdala had never read anything about Jews. She had seen people like him in the marketplace and at other occasions of state but she did not know anything about them. She assumed that they were a special kind of slave. Philip went on to explain, "We are treated like slaves by many people because we are different. They often harass us and call us names. My family migrated here long ago from the northern province of Bithynia, over 200 years ago. We were here long before the Roman Empire existed. Yet I am treated as if I do not belong here. It is safer and happier for me to farm in the country and stay away from the politics of the city. We have never been represented in the Senate and therefore we have few rights. Augustus has brought peace and life is good today, what it will be tomorrow we cannot know."

Many of the rich landowners had to tried to buy or force Philip to sell his small piece of land. It was only twenty-five acres but it contained a spring that was the source of water for all the rest of the farmers during hot, dry spells. Philip charged for the use of the water, but shared it willingly. Many of his customers did not want to pay for the use of the water. Over the years he had many scuffles with farmers and had to defend his property.

At long last his neighbors were leaving him alone. His four daughters were of marrying age and Philip was growing older and there would be no one to work the fields. It was just a matter of time before he would be unable to work himself. Nearing the gates to the farm, all four daughters ran out to meet them. All of them jumped into the wagon with the poor donkey pulling all of them home. Philip filled them in on finding Magdala and what had happened in the city. "Augustus is dead!" said Joanna. "Will that hurt us?" Philip winced. "I have this knot in my stomach that tells me it will."

Magdala moved in with Mary, Martha, Joanna, Salome and Philip. The cottage was small but very clean. It contained very little furniture so it looked much larger than it was. A huge fire glowed in the main room on the ground floor. To provide warmth and protection in the winter the house had been dug into the ground. The first floor was three steps down from the front door.

Magdala had never lived in such plain and austere surroundings. The daughters occupied two rooms upstairs and Philip slept in the main room. All of them decided that Magdala would be happy if she had a place of her own. The only spot left was a small room used to store firewood. Together they cleaned it. Salome went to the barn and found some of the left over wool and wrapped it in a blanket for Magdala. "Here try it

Magdala. It isn't fancy, but it is warm." Magdala curled up in the wool and immediately fell asleep.

Magdala began to adjust to her new life. There were no servants. They did not go to market to shop for food neither did they invite visitors to dine with them. In fact they rarely saw other people. Magdala learned how to manage a farm. She worked the fields, milked the cows, and chopped wood. She even learned how to kill a chicken or skin an animal and cook it. Because Magdala was so good at selling, Philip often took her to market with him. Sometimes they would take the vegetables to market out in the middle of fields where markets would just happen. Someone would set up a bench and then others would come and often there was a circle market created in a matter of hours without anyone planning it. Since Tiberius ruled, Philip and Magdala made the trip to Rome infrequently.

Magdala enjoyed the physical labor and some time to read and think. She missed her tutors and the wonderful books she had studied as a child. She was learning Hebrew and the ways of the Jews but their books were not enough for her, she wanted more. She missed the theatre and the poetry and the singing minstrels. Often, her mind went back to the day her sister Vestals were murdered. She felt guilty for being alive. She longed for the life of the city with all its smells and noise. The quietness of the countryside was invigorating but there had to be more for her somewhere else?

As Magdala matured, she looked more like a Jewess than a Vestal. In all of the years that she lived with Philip, none of them guessed that she was a Vestal, or so she thought. At the beginning of her eighth year on the farm, Philip decided that everyone should go to Rome. They would take two carts. The harvest was so great that he would need extra hands on the road. One of his neighbors agreed to watch over their farm while all of them took a holiday.

Happily they loaded the wagons and headed for the city. It took them two days to reach the gates, partly because they walked at such a slow pace and partly because the donkeys often refused to pull the wagons because they were so full. They were hoping that their cargo would generate a lot of money. They were looking forward to spending time exploring the city. None of them were prepared for the assault on Philip.

The Centurion's shrill whistle jolted Magdala back into the present. "And is that the highest bid?" he snarled. He was angry because the price offered for Joanna was so low. "One hundred drachmas, once, one hundred drachmas twice, one hundred drachmas..." Someone shouted,

"One thousand drachmas...." "Who offered that bid, let me see his face," questioned the Centurion. A very large dark-skinned man, wearing royal clothing of purple, stepped forward and offered, "One thousand drachmas!" "Do you have the cash on you?" asked an unbelieving Centurion. The man threw a bag of gold at him. "One thousand drachmas, is that my last bid?" shouted the Centurion as he held the gold before everyone to see.

Angry insults came from the crowd. They had been deprived of an execution and did no like it. The shop owners felt cheated. Some of them picked up rocks and began throwing them at Joanna. One hit the royally garbed dark man. "Can anyone match my bid," said the suspicious man. "If no will match my bid, then the woman is mine." The crowd grew more hostile. Some yelled, "Hey blackie how can a slave buy a slave? Yeah, how come you have more gold than we do?" The man slowly answered the seething crowd.

"I am Chusa, servant of King Herod of the East. If you choose to risk your life you will continue throwing those rocks. I command a thousand gladiators who are waiting for me at the edge of the city. Shall I summon them? Shall I call the gladiators?" Kicking and grumbling like a head-strong mule, the crowd began to slowly leave. Left behind were Philip who was barely breathing, Magdala, and the four daughters.

The Centurion took the 1000 drachmas from the pouch of gold, and threw it back at Chusa. "You are out of your mind. You could have bought a wench like her for one hundredth of the price you wanted to pay. You wasted your money. Calling to his aids, Chusa directed them to take Philip to his house and to find an Asclepioi priest to take care of his wounds. "The rest of you come along with me," said Chusa authoritatively. What else could they do? The man had intervened and saved Philip and Joanna from the crowd. Bewildered and afraid the five women followed the dark-skinned man through the city streets. Chusa stopped in front of a towering building on the north side of town; he invited them into the house. "Here, sit, and I will have food brought to you. Don't worry about your father, the Asclepioi will tend to him."

"Where have you taken our father," said Magdala. "You have no right to keep us here. We are not your prisoners. You did not purchase all of us." Chusa roared, "Listen to me, you ungrateful women. I saved your lives -- all of you--from that mob. Do you think that they would have stopped with killing your father? Mark my words; they would have murdered all of you in the same manner. I have seen this happen many times in Rome. Sometimes the mob turmoil turns into a wholesale

25

massacre.

"What are you going to do with all of us," cried Magdala. Joanna sobbed quietly while the others held onto each other. Chusa declared, "Joanna is mine. I bought her and she will go with me to Caesarea--in the East." "You can't take our sister away from us," whined Salome, the younger sister. "Listen to me, I am a Jew like yourselves. My mother was Jew who was taken by a Roman as a concubine. No one in the Roman government knows of my heritage. My mother died shortly after I was born while we were still in Egypt. My father, a Roman diplomat, brought me back to Philippi and there I was raised with full privileges of a Roman citizen." Salome retorted, "You don't look like a Jew and you certainly don't act like one."

"It does not matter what you think, I have purchased Joanna and she will live with me as my wife. She will learn to love me. I will be good to her. As you know, the ancient law states that every woman who is bought by a Jewish male must be treated as a wife and provide for her in everything she needs," argued Chusa. "Soon we will sail for the East. I offer all of you free passage on my vessel. Herod expects me to return soon. I must take care of his affairs at the southern palace, the Herodium. My own house is in Caesarea, which is on the coast of Judea. You are all welcome to stay with me until you find work and your own place to live. You may choose. Come with me or stay here. If you stay here, you may never see your sister again."

The daughters did not know whether they had been abducted or rescued. Should they believe this strange man? Why should he be so kind to them? What was he getting out of all of this? They were stunned. Meanwhile, the Asclepioi priests had attended to Philips wounds. Chusa inquired about his health. "The man is sleeping now. He will live but he has several broken bones. One arm was completed twisted backwards and broken in pieces. His left leg is broken in five pieces and may need to be amputated. It will take many months for him to heal, and he may never be able to walk. I must go to the temple immediately. I need to bring several herbs to help your father." Chusa asked the priest, "Sir, do you think that the High Priest would allow an Asclepioi priest to travel with this man to Caesarea?" "Yes, I have often traveled with people who are very ill. Once I even sailed to a land that they call the Mongols while taking care of a little boy with the fevers." "What is your name?" asked Chusa. "Some call me Lucas. I must go now, but I will return shortly. When do you plan to sail?" "Tomorrow!" Magdala stayed with Chusa while the four daughters went to their father. "Why did you stay with me," asked Chusa. "I am not of their family. I am only a boarder," explained Magdala. Chusa offered to take

Magdala also with him to Caesarea. Magdala, again, had no choice. She had no money, no clothing, and no means of travel. Her only alternative was to sell herself into slavery for a few years. She had to go with them.

Salome returned with questions for Chusa, "If we all go with you, who will take care of our farm, our cottage, our livestock? There is no one to feed the animals and tend the fields. Chusa pondered and then answered, "I will send some of my slaves to live on the farm. They will take care of it until your father is well enough to make a decision regarding the property. It is getting late and the ship sails tomorrow. In the morning you will have time to shop for a few things to take with you on the trip. I will leave a few hundred drachmas with Joanna. She can spend the money as she wishes."

Chusa showed them to their rooms and set a guard at each door. Close by, Philip lay unconscious. Had he been awake, things might have gone in a different direction. His fate and the lives of his four daughters were in the hands of Chusa. By the time he awakened and could feed himself, he would be in a foreign land.

Magdala's journey was leading her far away from her home and her past -- but only for a little while. She had royal blood in her veins and it would someday haunt as well as hurt her. It was a good day to sail. Magdala breathed in the ocean air at Ostia and looked across the sea. She did not know that she was sailing to the land where Lysander was born. Both of their lives would never be the same after they met.

CHAPTER FOUR
THE EAST. JUDEA
4 B.C.E.

"Poverty teaches some to be innovators and others to dream
incessantly."

Long ago a seeker, by the name of Abram, from a land called Ur
claimed that he had had a Divine visitation from a God by the
name of El. Together with his family he journeyed across the
desert to a country called Kinahni. According to the legend, El promised
Abram all the land he could see. He would become a master of a great
people who would one day conquer the earth. To his surprise he found the
land inhabited. Canaanites had built monumental shrines and huge walled
cities. From that day until this, Abram and his descendants have battled the
Canaanites for domination of the land.

From the springs of Dan to the wells of Beersheba, Judea expands
across desolate mountains and dry, parched valleys. Only to the north,
among the rolling hills of Galilee does the country provide continual relief
and refreshment from the hot desert sun. It is here, among the greening
towns, that Lysander gained great respect and popularity.

Mariam was on fire. Her heart burned for the young Egyptian,
Arman. Each day she would steal away from the fields to be with him. Life
had changed so much since his arrival in town. She was no longer a
peasant's daughter who must work in the hot sun for twelve hours a day.
She had become the concubine of an Egyptian Prince. For the past three
weeks she had spent her afternoons and evenings with Arman. Secretly
they traded stories underneath a towering Oak near the springs of Dan.
They were alone and no one in the world could tell them that they were not

royalty. Arman would speak of the Egyptian court and the huge stone peaks that whispered through the sands near the Sphinx. Mariam loved Arman. The brief moments that she had spent seemed like another lifetime. She forgot her rough, torn hands. They became the hands of a delicate and educated princess. She forgot her sun-darkened skin. It had been transformed into silk. She was beautiful for the first time in her life.

"Mariam, I have something to tell you," whispered Arman. "Tell me again about the tombs and the Valley of the Kings and the huge carved mountain called Abu Simbel. It sounds so wonderful. Oh how I wish I could see the sand shifting from one side of the Nile to the other," she chirped. "I have something to tell you, please listen, " said Arman. "What is it? Your eyes seem so sad. Have your parents found out about us?" asked Mariam. "No, they know nothing. They are busy with the politicians in Galilee. They don't even know that I exist. Listen to me Mariam, I have something very sad to tell you." Mariam was adamant, "Oh, don't ruin the day. Tell me tomorrow. Today is so beautiful. It is so good to be close to you, to feel your heart beating. When I hear your heart, I know that I am alive."

Arman attempted to explain, "Mariam, there will be no tomorrows." "And the world is going to end tomorrow, is it?" questioned Mariam. "No, tomorrow I am leaving." Mariam cried, "No you are not leaving. You must stay with me, here, what else could you ever want in life?" Arman continued, "My parents are leaving for Asia tomorrow and I have to go with them." In disbelief Mariam stunningly said, "No, no you cannot leave. We have shared our bodies, our thoughts, and our dreams. We have planned a future together." Arman chided Mariam; "You knew that we would only be here in the mountains for a little while. Why do you look so disappointed?"

Tears streaming down her face, Mariam stood up, turned around and began walking frantically toward home, "I am coming with you. I will go home and tell my parents that I am leaving for Asia tomorrow." Arman cried, "Mariam, you cannot come. Who would take care of you?" Wouldn't you take care of me, Arman?" "Mariam, I am only fifteen years old. How could I take care of a thirteen year old? It just would not work. Besides my parents would not allow it. We have customs you know and I have royal blood in my veins. I must be married to a princess of another country or someone with royal blood in Egypt. Of course, when I am older, I could take a concubine." Shocked, Mariam said, "A concubine? Don't you love me? And Arman answered sweetly, "I have loved each special moment with you. You have given me more love than any other person I have known or will know, but I must leave."

Arman's words crushed Mariam. Arman was everything that she had wanted in life. She had hopes that he would rescue her from the brutally hard work and take care of her. She could not let him leave, not now. "Arman, may I see you one more time before you leave?" Arman answered, "There is no time. We are leaving in the morning and I have to go back to the caravan." Mariam explained her plan, "I will come by early in the morning before you leave, before the sun. I will wait for you on the rise about the tents near the river. We can spend a few moments together. I cannot bear to say farewell right now." Arman conceded, "If that is what you wish. I will meet you but only for an hour or so. I do not want my parents to discover us." And they kissed. It was as sensuous and loving as any of their kisses. Quickly they parted without another word.

Mariam gathered a few things together back at her cottage. Everyone else was out in the fields tending the goats. She intended to escape her miserable life by stowing away in one of the wagons of the caravan. Arman would be with her forever. When they found that she had stowed away, she knew that Arman would tell his parents and then he would want her as his wife. The plan would work. Ready for her future life, she returned one last time to the fields.

Later in the evening, she went to bed early and arose some time after midnight. Quietly she made her way through the house clutching a small bag. In her haste she knocked over an oil lamp. "Mariam, is that you? "Yes mam, I have to go outside." Her mother warned, "Be sure to bolt the door when you return." "I will, mam, goodnight, I will be quiet." Holding her breath, she opened the door and ran down the path toward the tented village. It took almost an hour. Gasping and holding her chest, she reached the rise. It was so dark. Clouds covered the stars and moon. It was so dark but finally she saw the clearing at the bottom of the hill. Mariam screamed, "They are gone. The tents are gone."

Mariam, later in life, could not recall the days and months that followed. A neighbor found her sprawled out on the ground near one of the springs of Dan and brought her home. She could not speak a word. In fact she spoke to no one for almost three months. Her family did not know what to make of her. They talked with the local priest. He offered that it could be one of two things; either she was possessed by a demon or she had a divine visitation.

In the fourth month after Arman left, Mariam began mumbling about royal blood and becoming one of the Egyptian court. In the same month, her mother noticed that she was gaining weight although she rarely ate an entire meal. Mariam's mother, Ann, took her to the local Asclepioi priest who confirmed that she was pregnant. Ann was shocked, "Who is the father of this child?" Mariam answered shyly, "Arman, an Egyptian prince." "Mariam, there is no one around here by that name. Where did you meet this man? "He was traveling with the Egyptians," explained Mariam. Ann vaguely remembered the caravan coming through their village.

"When and where did you meet this Egyptian?" inquired her mother. I snuck off from the fields to visit the caravan. None of this made any sense to her mother, her father, or her brothers. They did not believe her and even laughed at her stories. Shortly, after discovering the pregnancy, Ann came to Mariam, "It breaks my heart to tell you this but your father will no longer allow you to live in this house. He will not speak with you. I have no power to change his mind. He cannot arrange a marriage for you with any of the local men because you are pregnant. You are an embarrassment to this family and have harmed the image of your father. He says that you are of no use to him any longer. You cannot work in the fields. He wants you to leave." But mother, "I have no money and no place to go. What will I do?"

"Find that Egyptian who got you pregnant and make him take care of you. Your father says that he has a little money saved for your dowry. You can take it and go to another town to live or find your lover wherever he lives," cried Ann. Mariam, crying too, "I have never been anywhere else. I don't even know where to go." Ann, with helpful advice said, "For the next few days you can visit your cousin d in the mountains. She is also pregnant and not feeling well. You can take care of her. You must leave now; there are rumors that the townspeople are planning to stone you. They say that you have been sleeping with one of the priests of the Moon. Take the money and go. Go quickly or you may never leave this house again."

Mariam made the journey up the mountains above Galilee to Isabel, her cousin, who welcomed her. Sacharia had sent Isabel to the mountain cabin because she was pregnant. He did not believe that he was the father of her unborn child. He was at least sixty and Isabel was only ten years younger. They were too old to have children. In all the years they were married, Isabel did not become pregnant. How could she be pregnant now?

Staying in the cabin together, Isabel and Mariam became great friends, or like mother and daughter. Isabel hoped to find Mariam work with local Roman officials but they did not want her because she was pregnant. After two months of looking for a place for Mariam, Isabel was desperate. Sacharia would not take care of two women with babies.

31

One day Isabel heard a knock at the door, "Tax Collector! Open up by the authority of Rome, Tax Collector!" Isabel opened the door and looked square in the face of the ugliest man she had ever met. He was old; at least she thought he was old. On top of his rather small stout body was a huge head covered with moles and shadowed by an odd-brimmed hat that had seen better days. Long grey hair covered most of his face except for a few prickly hairs protruding out of a few of the larger moles and his nose. In spite of his unseemly facade, his clothing was impeccably clean and neat.

"Hello," said Isabel. "Do you need something?" The Tax Collector barked, " I am here to collect taxes on this cottage. I recollect that you owe 700 drachmas. Now if you pay today, I will lower it to 650." Isabel did not know what to do; she did not have that much money. "I am sorry but my husband is traveling south with the herds. He won't be back for at least a month. Will you come back then?" "No," retorted the Tax Collector, "This is the fifth time I have come by this cottage in two years. No one ever seems to be at home. I must collect taxes or I will have to take your property. Now, I could be persuaded to take something of equal value for the money you owe the Emperor."

Tax Collectors were known to be unscrupulous. Each year Rome would levy a tax upon the whole district. Collectors would bid on the right to collect taxes about every two years. Whoever bid the highest amount of cash above the amount levied by Rome was awarded the contract. Their charge was then to visit every person in the district and extract as much money as they could from each person. The excess amount of money over that which was requested by Rome became the sole property of the Collector. Their tactics to obtain the taxes were often brutal and underhanded. Collectors could often become very wealthy.

"Do you have anything of value that you could trade for the taxes?" bargained the Tax Collector. This is only a summer cottage and its furniture is worth very little money. I do not have any cash. I am traveling back to Jerusalem tomorrow, will you wait until I arrive to collect the taxes," pleaded Isabel. Coming up the path from the river Mariam shouted, "Isabel have you finished packing?" She was startled by the stranger and turned around to run back to the stream below. "Mariam, don't be frightened. Come here child, this is a Roman Tax Collector whose name is...?" "Joseph, mam, Joseph is my name." "Mariam, come meet Joseph!" "Joseph would you like to have a cool drink and talk about the problems we are having?" Joseph was happy to be invited into the cottage out of the heat, "Thank you mam!" Ann asked Mariam to pour a drink of cool water for both of them. Mariam protested, " But Isabel...." "Go ahead Mariam, I will be fine in here with Joseph."

As soon as Mariam left the room, Isabel whispered to Joseph, "Do you have a wife?" "Why, no mam, I ain't so handsome and the ladies don't like me much." Isabel whispered again, "Do you want a wife?" "Well, I ain't really thought about it much. I be on the road so much and all but I do own my own house near Bethlehem and it could use a little woman to brighten it up. I hate to go to my house because no one I know lives there." Isabel continued, "What would you say to accepting a woman for the amount of taxes owed on this house?" "Why, there's a possibility that would work, " said Joseph thoughtfully.

Just then Mariam walked into the front room with drinks and sat down with Isabel and Joseph. "Joseph, this is Mariam, the person about whom I was referring." Joseph peered at Mariam with one eye and then the other. She squirmed in the chair. Looking down at Isabel he said, " Why she's only a little girl. She is a little girl who is having a baby." "So?" said Mariam, "what is so unusual about that? My mother was hardly my age when she had my little brother." Joseph looked at Isabel again, motioning with his hat, saying, "Can I sees you outside Mam?" "Surely, Mariam, Mr. Joseph and I have to talk outside. I will be back in a few moments."

The next day, Mariam found herself sitting on top of an old donkey heading south. Isabel waived good-bye. She would never see Miriam again. Isabel would be stolen by Herders shortly after the birth of her twins. Mariam had been sold to Joseph and became his prisoner. Joseph agreed to feed and clothe the child and her baby who was coming. Magdala felt nothing for the man but was happy that she would be taken care of by someone.

Joseph was very happy with his first and only woman in his life. Always a loner and always on the road collecting taxes, he had very little time to make friends or a family. Besides, the ladies claimed that he looked more like a monster than a man. But inside the monster's body was a sensitive loving child who longed to be loved. Mariam would experience this love over the next few years. Screaming, "Ah!!! Joseph something is happening to me. Urine covered the donkey as her water broke. I have pains in my stomach. I think it is time. " Joseph responded, "We be in the middle of nowhere. Bethlehem is up the valley about a day's ride. What can I do?" Mariam shouted, "Joseph, help me."

Next to the side of the road was an old cave where travelers camped. Joseph carried her over to its entrance and built a fire near the opening to keep animals away. Mariam struggled with the birth but he finally came. She was so young and small and the baby was many hours in coming. When it finally arrived, she looked at it and said, "One day you will save my life. One day you will bring happiness and prosperity to many people. You will be called Lysander." Joseph protested, "Lysander is a funny name for anything. Why don't you give it a regular name, like David or Joseph?" hinting that he would like the child to be named after him. "In the ancient religion of my parents, " said Mariam, "the name means protector or liberator. This child is the only thing that I possess on earth. I will be its protector and he shall be mine. His name shall be called Lysander."

Over the next few years, Mariam became a very secure and happy woman. Secluded in Joseph's rambling castle on the edge of the desert near Bethlehem, like two children, Mariam and Lysander played like brother and sister. Rarely did they venture into the countryside. They had everything they wanted inside the castle walls. Servants shopped and cleaned and took care of them all of the time that Joseph was away collecting taxes.

Lysander was the center of Mariam's life. Each day that she spent with him was like being with Arman. Although his fair skin and hair were unlike either of them, she could see Arman's chin. Within the protected walls of Joseph's home, time stood still for Mariam. Each day she would recall her romance with Arman and relive each ecstatic moment. Arman was the only man who had ever made love with Mariam. Joseph, took care of her, but he did not seem interested in having sex with her.

One evening while Joseph was out collecting taxes, after Lysander had gone to sleep, a courier arrived from Caesarea carrying a scroll signed by the Procurator of Judea. One of the servants read it to Mariam, "Joseph, tax collector for the State of Rome, was ambushed and murdered by bandits while on his way to bring levies to Rome. All of the taxes he was carrying were stolen." Mariam gasped, "How could this have happened? He left home with two mercenaries to guard the tax money. Go on reading." The servants read, "Joseph owes the State five million drachma. The State therefore is confiscating all of his assets, including houses, lands, furnishings, and slaves. These items will be auctioned off to the highest bidder on the fifth day of March. Signed, Pontias Pilate, Procurator and Chief Roman Administrator."

Suddenly, the doors and windows began to shake. There must have been fifty guards pounding on the walls. A Centurion called out in a very loud voice, "This house is confiscated for the State of Rome. All of its contents belong to Rome." Mariam ran to pick up her son and throw a few things in a basket. She had to leave before they discovered her. Quietly tiptoeing down the hidden entrance to the castle, Mariam grasped her son's hand and led him toward the dim light at the end of the tunnel. Breathing hard she reached the door and pushed it a little so that she could make a quick break into the hills. Out of nowhere came, "Halt, where are you going young lady? Think you are going to get away. You know what happens to runaway slaves, don't you? said a guard holding a spear and a sword. "I am not a slave, I am the wife of Joseph," shouted Mariam. "The State knows of no wife of Joseph. Do you have a paper to prove it?"

Mariam could prove nothing. Joseph had never legally married her. She did not think it was necessary. It was the custom among people, that if you lived with a woman for more than one year, that you were legally married. She had lived with Joseph for five years and explained it to the guard. "There's no law like that in these parts honey. Go back into the house. You will be sold with the rest of the slaves tomorrow. Don't even think of escaping. I have orders to kill anyone who leaves this house."

Mariam began to sob because she was alone again. She had no one to help her. Not even the servants could help her because she was to be auctioned off tomorrow too. Mariam cried all night long. In the morning the fields outside the house were filled with hoards of people, like vultures, ready to descend upon the castle. They hovered around the estate until the auction began."

A Centurion blew a loud horn and another Roman official began to speak, "The auction will proceed this way. We will sell the contents of the castle, then the slaves, then the castle itself." Mariam watched them carry away the furniture and the food and all the treasures that Joseph had collected over the years. Often he would take gold dishes or silver goblets as payment for taxes. Consequently his home was lavishly furnished. Soon it was all gone.

"Next the slaves, let's take the youngest first. Bring that little boy over here," shouted the Centurion. Mariam shouted, "What are you doing with my son? Do not take him. He is too little." She held onto to him as the guards tried to take him away from her. They were inseparable. The guards carried both Mariam and Lysander up to the top of the hill where the auctioneer was working. Someone from the crowd shouted, "Sell them both together. A child must be sold with its mother." According to the State, I must sell each slave individually, "said the Auctioneer. "I have no choice." Mariam howled, "No, NOOOOOOO! I am not a slave and neither is my son."

The bidding began. The Roman officials had no pity for Mariam and her son. They were simply property that was being disposed of in a legal manner. A family from Galilee bought Lysander. They were looking for a bright child to train to be their family physician. Buying someone so young was a good investment. The owners could train the child to become their household physician plus he would have the manners of the aristocratic class.

Distraught and at the point of exhaustion, Mariam was forcefully taken by the guards. Lysander was gone from her forever. Lysander traveled to the north, and there he was placed on a ship headed for Epidaurus, a city in Greece (Achaia). For the next ten years he would learn the ways of the Asclepioi.

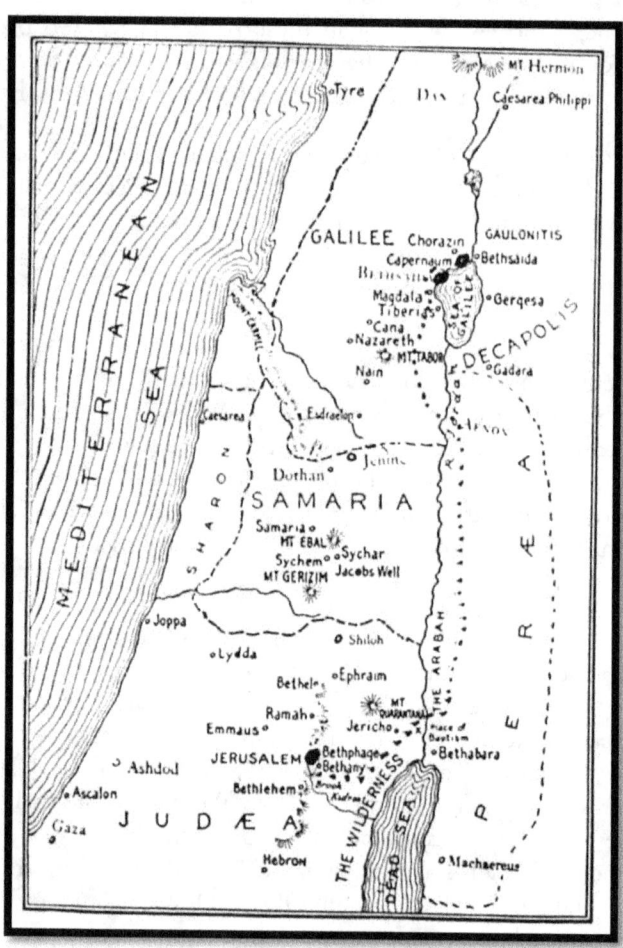

CHAPTER FIVE
THE BIRTH OF A MAGICIAN

"Healing like Sorcery is an acquired trade."

Asclepius, so they say, was the offspring of the God Apollo and a human. Apollo longed for Koronis, a Vestal Virgin. One night his desires led him to her bedroom where he attacked and raped her. Defiled and pregnant, Koronis searched for a man who would want her as wife. On the day that Koronis was married, in a jealous rage, Apollo blasted her with lightning. He spared his child born out of his unholy passion.

Asclepius, bastard child of Apollo, was sent to live with a Centaur who taught him the healing arts. In his quest for knowledge, Asclepius overstepped divine boundaries and unlocked the doors of immortality. As soon as Apollo heard of this dastardly activity, he disintegrated Asclepius instantly, hoping to protect the secret. Unknown to Apollo, Asclepius had already imparted the secret. Those who received this knowledge are known today as Asclepioi Priests and Priestesses.

Few apprentices pass the secret rites of the Asclepioi. Those that fail are banished to distant colonies along the farthest borders of the Empire. Lysander began his training at the age of six at the great temple in Epidaurus. His priestess-director, Hygeia, would serve as his mother, and later become his friend, companion, and lover. Before making his primary vows, and becoming a member of the community of priest-healers, Lysander had to pass the survival ordeal.

Two days after arriving in Epidaurus, Achaia, Lysander was

blindfolded and abandoned in a desolate mountain valley near the great shrine of the Oracle at Delphi. For seven days he would wander alone in the forests. If he survived then he would continue his education into the Asclepioi mysteries. Hygeia instructed him, "I will wait for you on the other side of the mountain. You must walk through the forest and scale the mountain in seven days. You will be given nothing. Your only protection must come from something within yourself. Be careful of the marsh and watch behind you at all times. Sleep with your back to a tree or rock. Watch the sun and follow it to the East and listen to the voice within. Are you ready?" "Hygeia, I want to go home," said Lysander, "I don't want to do this." "I know. But you have no choice, " answered Hygeia.

The ordeal tested the novice's inner strength, persistence, and endurance. If Lysander did not discover the strength and will to survive, then he could never learn the secrets that would bring health and life to others. He must learn how to protect and heal himself first. For the first time in his life Lysander was alone. The emptiness of being only with himself crept all around him. His body was frozen. Hours passed and he could not move. He wished that all of this would go away, if only his mother Mariam were here, she would make things better. Lysander was a little boy who had to face himself. By the next morning's warming sun he had found the courage to walk down into the valley. His search for food yielded nothing. So he began to walk and walk and walk. At day's end the night found a little boy trembling and crying at the foot of a huge crevice. He could not go on much longer without food or water.

On the third day, he was so weak that he could not tremble any longer. With tears in his eyes, he finally recognized the path that he had been walking. For the past three days he had been traveling in a circle. He thought that he would never make it across the mountain. Raising his hand toward the Gods, he noticed that it felt a little moist. Following this sign, Lysander tripped and fell into a spring near the edge of the mountains. He had found water, now he must find food. His eyes began to open. There were berries, and roots, and crawling insects, all of which could make a meal. He jumped for joy, "I can survive!"

And so Lysander learned the secret of the mountain ordeal. He listened to the voice within and was not afraid of it. Stretching out his arms, he made friends with the darkness of the forest by beginning a conversation with the plants and the trees. He was no longer alone. He had found a family of living things that wanted to help him. Without ever speaking a word to anyone, Lysander crossed the mountain and found Hygeia on the other side.

Lysander had begun the long journey of discovering himself. All at once he realized that he no longer mourned for his mother. Another living caretaker would always be in his life, the forest. He had discovered the life-giving presence of the Earth. Invincible and eternal, she would always be there to comfort and sustain him.

On the journey home, Hygeia, happy to know that her novice was succeeding, explained the vows that every Asclepioi must take. He would be expected to pledge his allegiance to the Gods and to never divulge the secrets of the mysteries. To this very day, no one really knows what happens during the testing time underneath the great temple at Epidaurus. All Asclepioi take a vow of chastity. They must never marry and all possessions belong to the temple. Lysander was encouraged to seek out a relationship with anyone who would make his life happier or healthier, but he would never be able to father children.

Lysander took his vows before thirty Asclepioi in his sixth year of life. "Come novice, come and make your vows to the healing God, Aesclepius. Come before this audience and recite your eternal message," said the great High Priestess. And so Lysander took his place before the narrow hall that led to the chambers beneath the temple. He looked at Hygeia and then looked back at the seething cauldron of scorpions. Speaking loudly, Lysander said, "Almighty Aesclepius, take this body and teach it the ways of life and the ways of immortality. Dwell in me and give me the power that will reach out to others. I promise total allegiance."

Lysander drank the first vial of potion that would make him sterile forever. "I will myself and my belongings to the temple until the day I die." Suddenly two large guards grabbed his arms and drug him over to the cauldron of scorpions. "What are you doing? Hygeia, what are they doing to me? You never told me about this?" And Lysander was correct. Hygeia did not inform him about the scorpion test. He would be bitten several times. And if he survived the poisonous bites and fever, a black spot would be etched on his left arm in the form of a snake. It was the sign of a healer. Screaming and fighting for his life, the guards pulled the little boy over to the kettle and thrust in his left arm.

Lysander's head began to swim. The marks of the scorpions stung his wrist. He began to shake and the fever came over him. When he awoke ten days later his hair had turned bright blonde and his left arm was black. The blackness would fade over the years but he would carry the scars with him until he died. Lysander emerged a different person. He had survived the second ordeal and how was being carried to the caverns below the great hall. This underground habitation would be home for him until he mastered all of the Asclepioi healing techniques. Some novices studied from three to ten years. Others faded into oblivion.

Since Lysander discovered the Earth and his own intuitive strength, his next challenge was to discover his body and mind. The voice from within had to be amplified. One by one the priestesses taught him physical-empathic skills. He learned how to divine the water and to breathe shallowly. Certain touches to the body brought certain responses. He used his fingers and then his arms. His right hand was always stronger and more effective. In extreme cases he was taught to use his entire body by lying with the victim or clutching the victim in his arms. He also learned how to use leeches and brews. The forest became a garden of remedies as he secretly dug for certain types of insects and berries.

One of the most unusual experiences was learning how to help a woman give birth to her child. The major skill was conversing with the unborn child. Asclepioi did not believe that babies should be thrust into existence in a violent way. Lysander learned how to coach both the mother and unborn child. He talked the baby into the land of the living. Lysander spent many years learning these secrets. Meanwhile Hygeia was always there. She encouraged him, chastised him, and practiced healing techniques on him. Among all Lysander's teachers, Hygeia was the most intriguing. Hygeia captured him in a way that he would never forget. Her intellectual abilities far exceeded his and she seemed to have a vast store of care for everything she did. In every healing technique or situation she was always in control.

Hygeia and Lysander, from the very beginning, lived together as family. Their daily necessities in their living quarters were taken care of by Asclepioi servants. The priesthood hindered no one from success. If a novice failed, it was because the novice chose to fail. By the time that Lysander had reached his teen years, his love for Hygeia had changed. He saw her beautiful long hair and meditated on her soft features. He wondered why he wanted to be close to her. Hygeia was also drawn toward Lysander. Being at least ten years older and having had other companions, she knew that she must wait for Lysander to mature. He must make up his own mind. During the time she was a novice, she had been assigned to an aging priest. And she had been given a choice. Since his death Lysander was her family too.

Hygeia waited until Lysander began to desire her. His desire was so great that it often interfered with lessons. One day, while practicing mind-healing and communicating techniques, Hygeia ventured, "Lysander, you can redirect the energy you are feeling toward me. That energy should be directed toward the ill, it should be used to heal someone." Lysander responded, "Hygeia, I think about you all of the time. I must overcome my feelings." Hygeia guided him, "Do not hide your feelings and do not overcome them. Let them live. Let them live and flower into whatever they will become." Lysander said, "I desire to touch you, to hold you, to be very close to you." Hygeia agreed, "And so I have desired you for so very long Lysander."

Clinging to each other, Lysander and Hygeia began a journey into another sanctum of the Divine. The fire within them would live. Their hands, eyes, and bodies had never known such pleasure and comfort. Their union brought both of them in touch with energies that are only given to a few. From that moment on, they no longer needed to communicate with each other through speech. Lysander would think something and Hygeia heard it and understood. This link would remain between them even when they were in different parts of the Empire.

Discovering and expressing his sexual desires facilitated Lysander in the mysteries of the mind. Having learned to look inside himself and redirect his own energies, Lysander was challenged to discover energies other than his own. With a keen eye, he developed abilities to sense other forces. In the process of detecting energies, one of his eyes would turn yellow. His vision began to change colors. Every person emitted a color, an aura. He began to read auras. When the aura was dark-green, he knew that his powers would not be effective. Sometimes combining auras could heal a person. If a person had a grey aura, someone with a blue aura might be asked to touch the ailing person at the same time that the Asclepioi priest touched all of them. Energies of immense quantity could be redirected by the priest.

Lysander cast spells, re-directed lightning blasts, and listened to the fire, wind, animals, and insects. When possible he used the art of dream therapy and helped cure people who could not sleep. By talking with their minds he could often heal physically ill persons. Sickness of the soul was a different matter but Lysander learned telepathy and mind-cleansing techniques. Health came to a very ill person after he applied both his mind and body strategies. He was usually successful. Sometimes Lysander was too successful. Healing became too easy for him. There were times that he caught himself applying the body or mind techniques without engaging his soul. He was like a box full of healing energy that had no heart.

The next skill was among the greatest. Lysander must learn how to talk to the dead. Only the dead and the Gods knew the mysteries of the immortality and eternity. Sitting on a flat stone near the temple fire

Lysander contacted the dead. Peering into the abyss was a frightening experience. This Netherworld offered only a grey experience and grey speech. To Lysander's surprise, he had to converse with this Netherworld alone. Hygeia trembled as she watched from the other side of the fire. Hygeia was afraid and stayed to watch the first few minutes of the ritual which was forbidden. The High Priestess ordered her to leave several times. She wondered, "What would he have to trade for the secret of immortality?" Hygeia had traded all of her unborn children. She wondered if she would ever see Lysander again? Some novices had given into the dictates of the Nethers and were sucked into their abode to live as slaves. Peering into the fire, Lysander, conjured up the deep. He whispered the magic words, "Makeo, exolambano, klaio, makairos kai apothanein." Messengers from the Netherworld came to meet him. "You must come with us. We will take you to the Nether City where all the non-living things abide."

Hygeia felt Lysander scream. Fear had gripped him because he did not understand what was happening to him. Hygeia knew. All Asclepioi priests and priestesses knew. Falling through the worlds, Lysander found himself in a space that had no end. There were no buildings and no walls. Colorless creatures came into his vision and then disappeared. It was like being in the dark and yet it was like being in a place where you were blinded by the sun. He could see very little yet he could see everything. He found himself before a group of creatures sitting in a circle of space.

"Welcome to our space," cried one of the beings. "All of us were once part of the colorful living. Now we abide here by choice. We have allowed you to make the journey because we think that you might want to join us. So many of the Asclepioi novices have become one of us." Lysander was puzzled. Was he really talking with the beings of the Netherworld or was it only a dream? Lysander began to speak, "I have requested a council with you in order to find out the secrets of immortality. Why have you brought me here?" The beings responded in unison, "We do not negotiate with many from the world of color. We have been noticing your progress over the past few years. You often healed without using your heart. You are indeed a candidate for our world."

"How do I find the secret to living forever," retorted Lysander. "That power is only given to those who join our ranks or trade something of value for the secret. We will give you the secret if you stay with us." Lysander responded, "That makes no sense. How could I help others or myself to live forever if I stay here?" "If you stay here, you can reach out to those you choose and bring them into a state of immortality. You can even use other people who live in the colorful world to help you. Once in a while you will be allowed to appear to those you have chosen. Of course your world would appear without color. You will be a God, in the sense that you will control a part of the universe that is assigned to you. Sometimes Gods must be eliminated because they fail in their assignments. We would give you an assignments and teach you how to use your powers," explained the Nethers.

"Are you telling me that you control all space and time," asked Lysander. "Yes, of course we do, but there is always the threat of other Gods from other systems that invade our time and space. They challenge us. So far we have always succeeded in protecting the colorful world," continued the Nethers. Lysander thought for a moment and then asked," "What do I have to do to become a Nether?" "You merely have to wish it. We will empower you then you must stay here with us." Lysander thought about Hygeia. How could he leave the world he knew so well for this nebulous abode in space? He could not do it. He would go back to the land of color. But he wanted both, immortality and his life. "I cannot become one of you. But I do want to know the secret of immortality. It would be a very useful tool." The Nethers answered, "For this secret you must pledge something of yourself, " explained the Nethers. "I own nothing, I can not give you anything material," negotiated Lysander. "You could give us a part of your future, your life." "What do you mean?" quipped Lysander. For this secret we would require you to give up your life in the colorful world for ten years plus the time needed to teach you the secret." "But that is so much of my life. I am so young, only eighteen years old. I do not know how to choose," cried Lysandra. "Then you will never receive the secret of eternal life or immortality."

"I must have it. Without it I am only a healer. I want to follow in the steps of Asclepius, I want to live forever. I must know the secrets so that I can help people in the colorful world, " mourned Lysander. "I will not choose the time. You choose and I do not want to know when it will happen," cried Lysander. The next thing that Lysander remembered was the temple fire. It had gone cold and Lysander was sitting on the slate floor in front of it. He remembered nothing but he felt a certain happiness. Holding up his hands, he was startled to see wrinkles. They looked older as if they belonged to someone else. As he stared into the copper pot he saw the face of an older man. His face had changed and his long golden hair now hung down to his waist. What had happened to him?

Lysander did not know that the Nethers had kept him in their world for over ten years. It took him that long to learn the secret of immortality. For Lysander it seemed like only seconds. He remembered only the grey lifeless space. The Nethers had erased everything about the Netherworld from his mind. In reality, the Netherworld was more splendid than anything the colorful living could imagine. Those that learned the secrets of immortality would stay in the colorful world. Those who did not would go to the Netherworld, a more perfect existence.

Lysander stood up and looked around. The temple furnishings had changed. He began searching for Hygeia. As he ran throughout the compound, an old Asclepioi servant ran into him. Lysander asked, "Have you seen Hygeia?" "Who are you?" The old man noticed the black arm and yellow eye and asked because he did not know anyone who had recently made vows to become a priest." "I am Lysander." "Lysander? Lysander, why we thought you had been taken by the Nethers. Where have you been all of these years?" Answering, "I have been in front of the temple fire. I began conjuring only minutes ago, I guess the magic did not work." Astonished, the old man said, "Lysander, you have been gone for years. You will find Hygeia in the same quarters, but beware, you will find something else."

Lysander ran to what used to be their quarters. Coming out of their room was an older woman. "Hygeia, Hygeia is that you?" asked a dazed Lysander. Hygeia looked up and saw the face of someone who seemed very familiar. Behind the long hair was someone she had known long ago. Lysander reached out to her with his mind. Instantly she knew. "Lysander is that really you?" "Yes, it is. What happened? I am still not understanding all of this."

Hygeia began to tell a story, "You have been gone for over ten years. We all assumed that you would never return. I nearly went insane when you did not return. The couple who purchased you gave up looking for you. You were to be their physician. The other priests and priestesses had to use all of their magic just to keep me from following you. It took me over five years to stop searching for you. I mourned every day and had no energy to heal anyone, not even myself. Finally the High Priestess assigned another novice to me. Magus has made up for the emptiness I felt for you."

Lysander's mind began to tear. How could all of this happen? How could he have lost Hygeia? She was the only person who mattered to him. She was family. "After you left, " Hygeia explained, "the High Priestess exorcized you from my memory. It was the only way I could have survived. We were bonded together. Now I am with Magus. We have a good life together and have hopes of traveling east. He has done well and will be on his own soon." Hygeia remembered Lysander but the fire had left her. Lysander had lost her. Could he ever win her back?

The truth was that she was gone. How could he have known that he was giving up this person who meant so much to him? It seemed like the Gods were playing a game with him. He sat down on the steps to the entrance to Hygeia's quarters and began to weep. His arrogant quest for immortality had left him all alone. Since she was gone, he would continue with the preparation. He hoped that something would change, but in his heart he knew that Hygeia was gone. He could no longer touch her with his mind.

Alone again, he had one last test to face and that was the test of immortality. Loneliness was nothing compared with immortality. He had to demonstrate his power over death. He was the same person who left ten years ago. Perhaps he only dreamed that he had learned the secret of immortality. His test came one day, late in the evening. As he returned to the temple after a day of healing in the streets of Epidaurus, a young woman came to him in tears carrying a beautiful little girl. A Cobra and its young had bitten the child. She had several bites on her face, hands, and arms. "I did not know that this had happened until late in the day when I came home and found her lying in front of the house," said the troubled woman.

Lysander listened to her heart. It was silent. "Your child is dead. Her heart has stopped," Trembling, the woman cried, "No, it can't be. She can't be dead. Hold her again and listen." Lysander took the child into his arms; tears also fell from his eyes. The child was so young, so perfect. "She is gone. I am sorry." Lysander tried to give the child back to her mother. "No, you can save her. Are you not an Asclepioi?" Lysander wished that he could give her life. He was not a God. He was only a novice serving Asclepius. He wished with all of his heart that he could help her. Suddenly the light around his face began to change from yellow to red. He picked up the child's body. It was cool to touch and her eyes were lifeless. He kissed her and said, "Anabaino, ercomai, zaw, live, live, live." And just as quickly the child began to move. Lysander had raised the child from the dead with his new powers. "Here she is, your child, take her home and bathe her and put her to bed." The young woman exclaimed, "You are a God, thank you!"

Slowly Lysander adjusted to the new powers within him. Months went by and the day finally came when Lysander was to make his final vow to Asclepius. He had passed all the ordeals, spoken with the Nethers, and now was looking forward to a life of service to Asclepius. Standing once again before the High Priestess, holding a staff, he swore before Asclepius and all other priests and priestesses, "To Asclepius I dedicate my skills. I will only use these skills to help and heal the weak and helpless. I will never use them for myself." This time Lysander walked to the cauldron and thrust his left arm into the pit. He believed he would not die. The sign was complete. On his left arm, the black sign of the snake appeared. He was now an Asclepioi priest.

The next day Hygeia waved goodbye to her novice and lover Lysander as he sailed to Judea after almost twenty years in Epidaurus. When he arrived in Capernaum, a long day's journey north from the port at Caesarea, no one was there to greet him. The family who had purchased him so long ago was gone. Some said that they had been killed at sea. Lysander sat down on the last step of the temple and brooded. He took a stick and began to write out his love for Hygeia whom he had lost. The temple had no room for another Asclepioi. He was told to back to Epidaurus. That was impossible because he had no money and had no means of obtaining any money.

While Lysander sat there, playing in the sand and pondering his life and future, homeless street children began to tease him. He noticed that one of them had a deformed leg and he had to hop on one foot. While the child was sitting in his lap, he reached over with his blackened arm and touched it. Immediately it straightened. The children were amazed and ran all over town telling people what had happened to the little boy. Some of the townspeople came out to meet him and invited him to stay in their homes. Lysander did not refuse. He went into town and accepted a bed in the local tavern.

News of his ability spread like a raging storm. When he arose the next morning, people were gathered outside the tavern. Some had stacked up food, others handed Lysander coins when he came out to meet them. He helped everyone who came to him that day. They marveled at his healing ability. Little did he or they know that someday those very people would attempt to crown him King of Judea.

CHAPTER SIX
THE DEADLY DISEASE

"Caesarea, Herod's bloody hands fashioned this city."

Caesarea Maritima was a coveted outpost on the western coast of Judea. Every military officer in Rome requested duty in this sparkling city. Tyche, the Goddess of good fortune seemed to smile on all of its inhabitants. Out of the ruins of a forgotten castle, Herod the Great took his own personal fortune and created a city in honor of Caesar. He built a harbor where there had been none, and raised pillars from the earth that became theatres and gardens. From high above the city, miles away, he crafted aqueducts that nourished and sustained the inhabitants of Caesarea. The desert blossomed.

Caesarea became the gateway to the East. Its marble streets and beautiful statues charmed citizens from every point of the Empire. Through its doors Roman military power exercised control all the way to the Persian Gulf. For many that calculated might encouraged unjustifiable savagery. Magdala would soon experience this unrelenting brutality.

Caesarea had a history of violence. Although Herod gave life to some, in paranoid frenzies, he took it from others. Fearing the ambitions of his own children, he murdered all of them. One night while his darling wife slept, he stabbed her to death. Like the fearful Herod, Caesarea was becoming paranoid. It feared the people within its borders and so occasionally turned on itself.

While Lysander battled the Nethers, Magdala sailed with Philip for Caesarea. Chusa had become their benefactor. His charming goodwill offered hope to Philip's family and a position in the Migration office. With the manners of an aristocrat, Magdala conversed in several languages. After only a few days in Caesarea, Magdala found herself at a table interviewing migrators from other countries. Many of these people lived on the edges of the Empire and coveted Roman citizenship.

Philip and his daughters did not fare so well. Most recently the Roman administration secretly decreed that the government would hire no Jews. There had been isolated riots throughout Judea and the Romans believed that the Jews were at the source of all the violence. In their well-ordered and splendid world of pageantry and pleasure, the Romans never forgot or forgave anyone who hindered them from serious play. While Philip and his daughters lamented their poverty, at the same time they enjoyed the company of many other Jews. The Jews were the main suppliers of food, cloth, jewels and medicine. In an uncanny way, every day the Jews and the Romans recognized their power over the other. Without the peace created by the Romans, the Jews would have no market.

As a symbol of displeasure and hostility toward the recent price-fixing by the Romans, the Jews staged a protest by boycotting the city. In fact Jews from all over Judea began to boycott Roman ports because of the Roman control of the economic system. They wanted more representation in government and control over the pricing of their goods. No one wanted to be told where to sell his or her goods, where to place their wares, or even which God to worship. In a reaction to the stern social-economic measures and the arrogant way the new measures were enforced, the Jews staged this boycott to demonstrate to the Romans how little power they had in Judea, and especially Caesarea. These revolutionary activities were not successful. The Romans despised seeing their weaker side. With one violent vote in the assembly they passed laws that prohibited anyone of the Jewish faith to be employed in government.

Meanwhile, Chusa's generosity comforted all of Philip's family. He had arranged for the servants to pack most of their belongings from the cottage. And all of it arrived safely. Through Chusa's neighbors, Philip met many Jewish artisans and shopkeepers. Times were not good. Philip thought that they could not stay in Caesarea for very long. He had to find work. Magdala's luck was so much better. Her relationship with the Romans at the Migration center was improving. She had successfully solved several international problems by bringing both sides to a compromise. Her aristocratic sensibilities delighted her Roman superiors. More and more the Romans began to trust her intuition and judgment about people coming and going in the Empire. Her only real problem was Philip. She heard about the ban on hiring Jews and did not want the administration to discover that she was living with a Jewish family.

One morning a local Roman official, some called him the Pontifix Maximus, sent for her. Fearing that they had found out about Philip, Magdala panicked. Arriving at his office, he began to question her. "Magdala, I understand that you have been running the Migration office across town. "No, Sir," Magdala answered, "I work for several officials. "That is not what I have heard. I heard that you make all of the major decisions for incoming migrates." "Sir, I make suggestions, only suggestions." The Roman continued, "Well, I have been ordered to request your services for a special assignment. The Procurator has had to deal with many violent eruptions this year. Most of them, as you know, are due to the economic and religious differences with the Jews. There is a group of people called the Zadokites living in the mountains near the Dead Sea. Many of us think that they are planning a military strike on Roman forces in the desert. We would like you to travel to their mountain retreat and discover their plans. You would be perfect for the job because you speak Aramaic and work for the Migration office."

Magdala answered, "I don't quite understand, Sir! What are you asking me to do? Are you asking me to spy on these people? "In a sense yes," explained the Official. "We need this information and would be willing to provide you with the things and people you would need. In exchange for your work we will offer you the position of Chief Administrator of Migration." Magdala breathed a sigh of relief. The Romans were unaware of her relationship with Philip. Her life was not in danger. She had thought that all of this was about losing her job. Instead, they offered her a promotion. How hard could it be? She would have to travel inland and interview a few of these people. From everything she had heard about them, they were harmless.

Within a few days, Magdala left Caesarea bound for the mountains. With her she took a caravan and about ten people and other military personnel. Most of them were Centurions who were commanded to protect her. Unknown to her, a legion of armed militia waited near Caesarea. If Magdala sent word back that the group was dangerous, they would attack and destroy them within days. Chusa heard of Magdala's assignment and was not happy about it. She had become an agent for Rome. He chided her, "They will ask you to more than just these interviews. If you are successful, you will be asked to do more dangerous types of missions. And you will not be able to refuse them." Magdala would not listen to him. This would be a great adventure. It almost seemed like she was back home in Rome, living as a Vestal, and being escorted through the streets. The mission was not dangerous, so she thought. Within ten days she would be visiting the Golden Temple and step inside the great walls of Jerusalem. She could not wait to step through its ancient gate.

Jerusalem was a city that almost shined. Its Golden Temple refracted light even outside the gates. Outside the stonewalls were miles and miles of orchards and farms of every type and description. The irrigated land was fertile and the city took away your breath. Stationed on top of the city walls were Centurions. The Romans claimed that this was their city. In front of the Great Temple was a pavement that spoke of power and invincibleness. Magdala felt very small as she walked through its doors. How could the strength she felt within this structure be conquered by anyone? Some said that it had taken ten thousand people about forty years to build it. For the Jew, it was the center of the earth. There was no escaping the message that the temple beamed to visitors. It would last forever, like the Earth, and everyone acknowledged it.

Magdala's caravan stayed within the city walls before heading south toward the Dead Sea. As she walked the streets people sang and danced and played instruments. How could these happy people threaten powerful Rome? It made no sense to her. She thought, "If I could choose a place in all the world to live, it would be Jerusalem. People from all over the Empire live in peace here. While Herod the Great built the Temple for the Jews, all people in the city were proud of it. You could see the pride in their eyes."

This assignment thrilled Magdala. Everything was new and different. She loved all the strange people and their ethnic dress. In her childlike zeal Magdala failed to understand the politics surrounding her. Many of the people she passed by in the street wished for her death. She represented Rome and the freedom that was lost when Rome conquered Judea. On the way to the desert, the caravan stopped by an Oasis near Jericho. Jericho was only a dust blown hill now, but stories about it date back before people knew how to write letters. On top of its ruins, people say, thousands of battles were fought between the Gods and invaders from other worlds. Today it is only a pile of rocks that seemed to grow smaller with every drop of rain or wind gust.

Magdala looked over the wasteland and thought to herself, "How or why would anyone live here? It is such an empty and forgotten space." She turned to the Centurion who had read her mind. "Miss, people only come here if they have no place to go. It is the best place in all of Judea to hide. Magdala asked, "How do people survive? I have seen tents on the mountainsides outside of Caesarea. Why do they choose to live in the desert?" The Centurion continued, "If you grow up in the desert, you know how to make your way. You know where to find food and water. You and I would not survive a single day in this heat without water. These people enjoy the heat and the hazards of the mountains."

Magdala thought that the Herders looked so interesting, she wanted to talk with some of them. "Miss, they look harmless but they are not. Many caravans have been lost in the desert. Some say that they are lost to sand storms; others think that they lose their way and die in wadis. Most of us think that the Herders prey on people while they are sleeping. If you don't protect your water, they will even steal it during the day." Magdala was alarmed, "You are telling me that these simple Herders steal and kill travelers?" The Centurion had finally made his point. "Yes, that is what they do so we don't need to be talking with them."

Magdala was happy to be surrounded by several strong and heavily armed Centurions. She thought she was safe. "One more thing, Miss. They have recently been slipping into Jerusalem at night and stealing women and babies." "Why would they do that, " Magdala insisted. "Most civilized women would not to live in the desert with the Herders. They have to force women to become their wives and bear children for them or their way of life would die out. The babies are taken for slave labor." In disbelief Magdala wondered, "This happens under Roman rule? Why do they allow it? I can hardly believe that this happens." "According to the villagers we visit, once a woman or child is stolen, they are never heard from again," said the Centurion.

Magdala was uneasy. The Centurion seemed to know too much about the Herders. He had a smile on his face when he told the stories. Magdala stopped the conversation. Maybe he did know too much about the Herders? Suddenly a courier that had been sent ahead of the caravan raced back to Magdala, "The Zadokite settlement is just over the hill." Magdala sighed. She would not have to face the thought of Herders attacking them tonight. Several older men greeted her in the valley near the meetinghouse. They were plain, quiet people, dressed in sand-colored robes. As far as she could see, they had no protection. What were they doing out in the desert? Why do they live in caves that could sustain no living thing?

Magdala looked around at the barren hills, not a single bush. High above the meetinghouse, in the middle of a cluster of hills, she could see several hundred men looking down at her. They must have been three thousand feet above her. An old man, known as the Elder began his story. "We are descendants and now brothers to the great Teacher of Righteousness who brought this group out here to the desert. Long ago our Teacher realized that foreigners and women had profaned the temple in Jerusalem. The ancient Jews did not build the magnificent structure that stands in Jerusalem today. It is not a holy place for us. We have come out to this place in the desert because we want to preserve the ways of the ancestors. For over one hundred years we have been copying ancient Hebrew fragments and texts as well as the poems written by our community. We have written a law book, the Community Rule, that explains how to become one of us, that is to live the life of an Essene in this Community of Zadokites, righteous ones."

Magdala was enthralled and so asked, "So you only admit males into the community?" "Yes, we only take males who promise celibacy. We believe our gathering will be more pure, more wholesome, and more holy without the presence of females." Magdala was familiar with this type of thinking toward females. She had heard stories from Philip's daughters about the place of women within the temple and other religious activities. The Zadokites were escaping many things and among them were females.

She asked the Elder, "How do you survive out here in the desert without food or water nearby? And, besides copying manuscripts, what do you do with your time?" The Elder was pleased with her questions and so gave her a tour of the compound. She had to promise not to touch anything or talk with anyone. He took her to the great cistern, one thousand feet below where she was standing. "Where did you obtain all of this water?" asked Magdala. "Look up above you, do you see troughs along the sides of the mountains. They look like rock ditches," explained the Elder. It rains, usually, only once a year. And when it rains the water is directed into this cistern. We have more than enough water for a couple of hundred monks to live several years."

Next Elder took her to a cave high above the desert floor. She was lifted up in a basket. There was no other way to enter the cave because the cliff went straight up the sides of the canyon, which had been hammered smooth by the rains and hit desert winds. The cave was dark and small. It had been hewn from the rock with a small rough instrument. Inside, stores on short tables of wood, were rolled manuscripts and torn pages from other writings. On the other side of the area were a blanket and a few dishes. No personal items, such as clothing or sandals were in the cave. She noticed a metal scroll sitting in the corner. "What is this? It is a special story that will tell the whole world about us someday. It is of no concern to you," said Elder in a huff. Turning around Magdala backed into a sword hanging over the entrance to the cave, "What is this and why do you have it here?" Sternly, the Elder said, "I will tell you about these later. Let's go down to the meeting house!" And so, one by one, two strong monks lowered them to the ground.

Next to the meetinghouse were a cemetery and a wading pool. Elder explained that all monks or initiates must wash daily. This makes them worthy of worshipping and being together in the community. It also prepared them for the coming of the Teacher. They believed that they would be resurrected like their Teacher. Together they would live forever.

A simple, flat stone served as a focal point of the Meeting House. It was the altar, Magdala guessed. One candle was placed in the middle of the stone and the other was lit and stood on the dirt floor. "You have water but where do you obtain food?" asked Magdala. "As you can see, we do irrigate and grow some things in a garden near the Cistern. But truly we could not survive if it was not for the generosity of our families and friends who believe in us. Most of our families support us. Others support us because they believe in our ways. Of course, all of us willingly contribute all of our own resources and inheritances when we join the community. That is part of the Rule. Come, let us dine together. She sat on one of the very low tables in the meetinghouse and the monks brought food for her and Elder.

Magdala enjoyed herself immensely. These peculiar men claimed that they did not like females but they treated her like royalty. While most of them were not allowed to speak to her, those that did were very interested in her life. Some of the silent ones communicated to her with their hands, or eyes, or by nodding their heads. They were excited to hear about Rome or Caesarea or any modern city where people lived. Many of the monks had been brought to the community when they were only a few years old. Their whole life had been spent on the mountain and in caves.

Magdala told them about the court life in Rome and news about the Empire. They seemed to be starved for knowledge about other human beings. Yet Magdala kept thinking that there was something wrong with everything she was experiencing. They were polite and interested but they were not telling her everything. Elder refused to discuss the swords that appeared to be resting or hanging everywhere.

That night after a wonderful meal of potatoes, greens, and chicken, Magdala collapsed into her tent that had been set up just outside the community. To her surprise, the next morning, she found a rolled manuscript next to her mat. She began to scan the Hebrew letters that foretold of a great battle between the Sons of Light and the Sons of Darkness. The rules of a future community were in a section called, The Future Congregation of Israel. What did all of this mean? What was she reading and why was it left next to her mat?

The scroll was not in the best condition. As she tried to unfold it, the bottom of it was flaking off. An animal had eaten part of what looked like and old papyrus scroll from Egypt. She had seen some of these in the temple in Rome. The handwriting was in Hebrew. She began to read about the Teacher of Righteousness who was sometimes called Mashiak and a belief that he would return after his death. The sons of Elder believed that they would rule the Empire and the world someday. She thought, "Rule the world? Those quiet pious men think that they will take over the governments of the world? That is the reason for all of the swords, they are planning a revolution?"

Trembling, Magdala carefully rolled the scroll back together and tied it securely with the old piece of cloth. Her first thought was to inform the Centurion but then she thought she would wait and collect more evidence. She would have a lot of time to decide what to do on the long journey back to Caesarea. At that very moment, the Elder appeared at the entrance to her tent. He had been called to Jerusalem and came to bid farewell to her. There was a problem with one of the novices who had been sent to the city to purchase food and other items for the community. Apparently he had visited a temple prostitute, lost all of the community's funds, and was arrested for assaulting one of the prostitutes. The situation demanded his presence and he had to leave within minutes. Elder apologized for the hasty departure and invited Magdala to return and visit again.

A summer sandstorm began kicking up as Magdala and the caravan headed back to Caesarea. Moving was slow and very dangerous. The drivers could barely see the road in the front of the carts. Many caravans had been lost in weather like this. Finally the sand was so thick that the camels refused to move, they just sat down and tucked their heads into their thighs. In a desperate attempt to save their own lives and the lives of the camels, the Centurions threw up a canvas over the camels and crawled into a small cave a few feet away. They tied the camels together and left them huddling in the makeshift windbreak. The winds howled for hours. At daybreak they peaked outside of the cave to discover that all of their provisions were gone. Without supplies they could never safely cross the desert.

They decided to stay in the cave until the storm had completely stopped. Suddenly they heard a chilling war cry from the top of the hill above the cave. Magdala was sleeping deep inside the cave and Centurions were stationed at its entrance. One by one the Centurions were dragged by several men and thrown down upon the rocks below the cave. Magdala could not see who they were? Where could she hide? She turned around to run but someone grabbed her arm and her long hair and began dragging her across the jagged floor of the cave. As soon as they passed the cave entrance, they threw her down. She looked up and gasped, "Herders!"

CHAPTER SEVEN
LOVE'S VICTIMS

"Never, never look into his eyes!"

Towering over her like a huge statue of Zeus, he offered his massive and dark hand. The rest of his body was wrapped in long pieces of cloth. She turned around and saw a crackling fire behind her. "Stop that, stop burning those things. They are not yours. Leave us alone," she yelled. Picking herself up, she ran toward the huge fire. Another Herder came up behind her and tackled her to the ground. With one great sling of her body, she landed in the fire. "God help me! Someone help me! I can't die now!" screamed Magdala as she tried to scramble out of the fire. Again, the Herder with the strong, dark hands pulled her from the fire. Unable to defend herself, Magdala lay face down in the sand sobbing. She was fresh meat for the Herders. She could see it in their eyes. They were looking at Magdala's soft light skin and long hair. They wanted her. One by one they began to walk toward her until she was surrounded. "What are you doing? Who are you?" asked Magdala.

Magdala did not know what was happening to her. While she had experienced violence and known of death, she had never experienced the raw desire of men who had been Herders all of their lives. Standing up, she shouted at them, "Who you think you are? I am special emissary for the Procurator of Judea. If you don't leave me alone, he will send a legion out to arrest you!"

Magdala kept screaming and they kept getting closer and closer to her. It seemed as if they could not hear nor understand her. All of a sudden she understood that they spoke a different language. She screamed and screamed and ran toward two of them to escape into the desert. Like hunting an animal, the men let her break free only to run after her. Daylight was fading. She might have a chance of survival if she could find a cave or lose them in the dark.

She ran and ran until she came to a huge lake they call the Dead Sea. Diving into the water she held her nose and went down deep into the water. But she had to come up for air, and when she did, something hit her in the head and she fainted. The next morning as she awoke she found herself under a sheep's skin. The stench of it was sickening, tiny creatures were crawling all over her. Jumping up, she headed straight for the door of the tent. A very tall dark-skinned man stood at its entrance. Magdala screamed, "What am I doing here? You can't keep me here? What are you doing? Where are my clothes? These filthy rags are not mine!"

In perfect Greek, the dark-skinned man answered her. "Hey little girl, how did you get that bump on your head? Magdala answered, "I don't know. Something hit me just as I was coming up for air. Who are you and why have I been taken prisoner?" "Do you remember all of those Herders that were chasing you out in the desert last night? "Yes, vaguely," mumbled Magdala. "There would not have been much left of you today if I had not caught up with you first. They have never touched a woman with skin like yours. All of them wanted you and they all would have had you if I had not stopped them. I spent most of the night challenging and fighting them in order to save your life," explained the man. "Look at my face and arms!" Magdala thought that he looked like he had been in a fight with a mountain lion. "I killed many of them and brought you back to my tent. The fire had burned your clothing. I threw the charred pieces away and dressed you." Magdala asked, "What are you going to do with me? Can I go now? What happened to all of the Centurions? Where are they?" The questions overwhelmed the very weak man. With falsehood in his heart, he said, "They are being held at another village. I will take you to them when I am well."

Unknown to Magdala, she was the only survivor of the attack in the desert. The rest of her companions had been stripped and left dead on the desolate rocks far above the Dead Sea. All of her supplies, clothing, and arms had been divided among the Herders. The scroll that had mysteriously appeared at her head the night before was thrown into a cave with other loot that the Herders had stolen from caravans. Magdala silently scanned the dark-skinned man. Was he a Herder too? He was young and healthy and did not speak or act like the other Herders. Although his skin was dark, he did not look as weathered like the others who spent their entire lives in the sun and on the sand. His eyes were like pools of darkness. As she stared at him, she felt herself fall into the darkness. He was strong, articulate, and handsome. They called him, Bara.

Bara had studied Greek in Cilicia, a Roman city, and had been abducted by the Herders when he was only a teenager. His family was vacationing south of Jerusalem when the Herders took him as a slave. Over the past ten years he had fought his way to a place of leadership among the Herders because of his strength and intelligence. He had learned the Herder's language very quickly and then used it to barter for his tribe with other Herder tribes and caravans that passed through the desert.

Under the watchful eye of Bara, Magdala began to recover. While she slept in the tent of Bara, he never made any advances toward her or suggested that she owed him anything for saving her life. She was free to walk the fields and talk with other Herders and their women and could leave the settlement in the desert to walk to the sea. No one ever stopped her. Strangely, she never met any women her own age. There were a few little girls and many older females but never any younger women. So she asked Bara, "Are there no other young females in your tribe?" Bara hedged and then said, "You are the only one." Magdala answered in disbelief, "That cannot be true. There are young children everywhere. Where did they come from?" Bara answered, with eyes twinkling with a tinge of fire, "We steal them. We take children that we think could survive the life of a Herder." Magdala kept prodding him, "But you are not a Herder! You were captured. Why don't you leave? You seem to be stronger and healthier than all of the rest. Why don't you go back north and find your family. Don't you miss them?" Bara answered, "I cannot go back. There is nothing there for me. I only have what you see before you," as he pointed to the tent and other Herders.

Magdala kept at him, "How do you know that there is nothing out there for you? You could live in a more civilized world. You could learn a profession, you could...." Bara cut her off sharply, "I have nothing and that is the end of that subject." Magdala did change the subject, "Do you feel well enough to travel? I would like to be going home now. My friends will be worried about me. I am sure that the Migration office expects me to report back any day now. Is there any way that I could send a message by a courier to them?" Bara answered, "I am not ready to travel but I would be most happy to send a message by way of the next caravan through the mountains. Another market caravan should be here tomorrow." Magdala jumped at that idea, "But Bara, I could go with them if they are heading for Jerusalem. From there the military could escort me to Caesarea." Bara explained, "No caravans will not be safe. I will return you to your home myself. I know the ways of the desert peoples. Your life will be more secure with me. But you can choose, if you want to risk traveling with the caravan. I will not keep you here against your will any longer."

Magdala did not know what to do. She did not want to be ambushed again. Bara seemed so safe and he did promise to take her home. She decided to wait a few days and travel with him. Locating a well-used piece of animal skin, a pen made from a small twig, and crushed berries for ink, Magdala wrote of her capture and safety while gently assuring her superiors that she would be home soon. They must reward the man who saved her life. She would be traveling with him and the other Centurions within a few weeks. Magdala handed her letter to Bara who stuck it in the pocket of his robe. Bara stared into the fire as he read Magdala's letter and then stood up and threw the precious message into the flames. Little did Magdala know that Bara, the man who saved her life, was chief of all the Herder tribes.

Meanwhile outside the tent where Magdala slept, Bara gathered some of the Herders. They were complaining to him, "Bara, we need to move on. The grass is almost gone and the goats need water." Bara agreed, "We will go tomorrow. Let's head west toward Beersheba. I have heard that the summer has not been so dry there. We will walk on the western side of the mountains where we will find a few springs of water. Break camp in the morning and bring the others. Place the women and children at the back of our caravan.

The next morning, Bara awakened Magdala early. He assured her that they were heading toward the coast, west and then north to Caesarea. As they began their journey, Magdala knew that they were not headed for the trail back towards Jerusalem. They were heading south. She confronted Bara, "This is not the route to Caesarea. Where are you going?" Bara attempted to cover his lies, "Magdala, we must take a route near the mountains that will protect us. We will travel south and then west before we head north. We must find other Herders in order to strengthen our tribe. They will be waiting for us at the wells in the south. As soon as we find them, we will also find your Centurions."

The story seemed logical to Magdala, yet she wondered at Bara's smile. So Magdala decided not to worry and tried to enjoy living with a different people and learning their language. She ate and slept in tents and constantly complained about the lack of water to bathe. As they journeyed, the days turned into months, and she grew to admire Bara more and more. She trusted him. Home did not seem so urgent as it once did.

One evening while Bara and Magdala sat by a small fire, she began to look at him with eyes that she had kept hidden. " Bara, don't you have a wife?" Bara answered, "No, I have never married. It is hard to find a woman who would live the way I do, with the herds." Magdala looked at him and wondered how such a strong and intelligent man would choose the way of the Herder. "Why don't you come back with me to Caesarea? I am sure that I could persuade the administrators to give you a position. Your Greek is excellent."

Bara had been patiently waiting for this moment. He sensed that Magdala was falling in love with him. He reached over towards her and gently kissed her. Magdala was startled. She realized that she had worshipped Bara since the moment he saved her life during the raid. Feeling of both appreciation and fear often arose inside her. She was conflicted. She believed his words with her mind but her heart sensed something was wrong. Bara kissed her again.

Falling into his arms brought tears to her eyes. She allowed all of her fears of the past few months to come upon his shoulders. She gave into his wishes and trusted him. Her heart was opened to this unknown person. She did not realize how much she was risking. Within minutes, Bara carried her into his tent. It had been her tent too for the past months. She never asked him where he slept, it never occurred to her to ask. She just assumed that he was sleeping in another tent.

So Magdala fell into the dark abyss of Bara. She opened her heart and body to his touch. She gave and Bara touched something deep inside her. She had never slept with a man before this night. Philip had protected her from everyone. In Caesarea, she had very little opportunity to socialize with males. Perhaps her training as a Vestal had something to do with all of it. She never noticed the smiles and desires of the men around her. She was dedicated, honest, and so naive.

Magdala understood Bara, so she thought. With every touch she enjoyed him. They were comfortable and happy together. Soon they would travel north to Caesarea where they would both have a better life together. Her enjoyment of Bara was the most important thing to her now. Questions about directions and intentions of their travel seemed to be unimportant. She feared that they would arrive at her destination too soon and this happiness she felt would end. So they traveled together for about another week until one day when Bara burst into their tent, "Magdala, where is my food?" Startled Magdala replied, "Where is your food? Haven't they brought it yet? I don't understand?" Bara grunted, "You should be preparing meals for me." Magdala surprised, "I should do what? Bara, I do not know how to cook Herder food." Bara shouted, "Take off those clothes and put on this robe." Magdala had been wearing clothing that Bara said had been bought from a caravan. They were too large for Magdala but they made her feel more civilized than the rags she wore right after the attack. Bara handed her a black heavy robe and veil. "Put these on." Magadala complained, "Bara, this robe is too heavy and it drags the ground. It was made for someone twice my size. It is too hot to wear and why would I wear a veil?"

With one huge sweep of his hand, Bara came back and hit Magdala across the face. The bolt thrust her to the other side of the tent. Her cheek was bleeding. "Bara, what is the matter with you? What is happening?" With his other hand he hit Magdala again and knocked her down to the tent floor. "Woman, never question me. I am your master and you are now my concubine." Magdala tried to argue with him, "You are not my master." And Bara hit her again and again and enjoyed every minute of it. "If you do not obey me, I will bring in the staff and you will learn how to obey like the goats." Shaking, bleeding, and sobbing Magdala did as he requested. Unknown to Magdala she was putting on the garb of a Herder's concubine. Crouching in the middle of the tent, she tried to wash her wounds as she lay sobbing and throwing up at the same time.

Bara did not return that day. When she walked outside the tent, no one would look at her. Her face and arms were swollen from the beating but no one could see because she wore the robe and veil. She bent down to take a drink of water out of one of the jars of water. And old woman pushed her aside, shaking her head. The others grabbed her and forced her back into her tent. She had become a prisoner.

One very hot afternoon Bara returned. He came to the tent and grabbed Magdala. "Come with me!" A frightened Magdala questioned, "What is going on? The Herders will not share their food and water with me. I had to eat with the animals this past week." Thunder hit Magdala as Bara swung his huge hands and hit the back of her head. "Come with me!" Dutifully she followed him to a camel outside of the tent area. With stern dark eyes, he ordered, "Follow me!" "Bara, please help me climb up the camel." Bara took his whip and began to hit her hands as she tried to scale the animal. She fell back to the ground." Follow me. Walk and follow me. And so Magdala, wearing a heaving black robe and a veil that concealed her face, followed Bara into the desert. He rode the camel and she tried fervently to keep up with him. She thought that this was a dream, how could this be happening to her? She hoped that she would awaken soon and find herself safe at home with Philip and his daughters.

Sun-parched and hungry, Magdala looked up at Bara and pleaded, "Please, some water, please." He ignored her and rode all the faster. It seemed as if she was running for hours. All of a sudden everything went blank for Magdala. She awoke in the middle of several faces looking down at her, kaying naked in a wet sheepskin. Bara had been leading her to his Serai and on the way she fainted from heat exhaustion and dehydration. Some of the concubines rescued her and were trying to cool her overheated body. "Where am I? What is happening? "Give me my clothing. Let me out of here. Let me out of this place right now."

Magdala was delirious and kept kicking and biting the women. In order to protect themselves, they tied her feet and hands to stakes and pounded them into the ground. For days she lay in this condition. Fever and stupor alternated. Finally she began to sleep. One evening a young woman leaned over to Magdala, "Hello, are you okay?" This was the first voice that Magdala understood. The young woman was speaking Latin. Before her stood a ten year old ragged little girl. "Hello Miss, are you okay? Can you hear me? You have been lying here for so long, I wondered if you were still alive?" Magdala tried to sit up but the ropes held her down. "Would you help me? Please help untie my hands, little girl," Magdala asked. "Do you know why I was brought here?" The little girl also asked, "Are you not like the rest of the women here? Are you not a concubine?" Shocked, Magdala answered, "A concubine? No, I am not a concubine, I work for the Roman government."

The little girl went on, "Well, you are being treated like one of the Serai. The rest of the women are out in the fields or tending the goats and sheep on the hill. Over the past two weeks I have been taking care of you. I like doing it too, it's better in here, I hate the hot sun." Magdala asked, "What do they call you? "My name is Tabitha. That has always been my name, I think?" "And your name is Magdala, you are one of Bara's concubines." Tabitha explained, "I heard the others talking. They said that you belong to him. He has about twenty concubines that do all of the work for him." Magdala screamed, "No! I am not his concubine. Help me find some clothes so that I can discover a way out of there." Tabitha again had to explain, "The only clothing you may wear are the black robe and veil that signify that you are a concubine. And you better take care of those because the other women will steal them from you. I hid them for you the first night that you arrived. You know, we thought you were going to die."

Weakly, Magdala put on the rags and headed for the tent door. As she reached for the opening to the outside world, she collapsed. Tabitha helped her into a mat at the back of the tent. She gave Magdala a word of advice, "You know, if you were smart, you would pretend to be sick as long as you could. When you regain your strength, they will put you out in the desert to harvest cactus plants." Magdala complained, "They can't do that to me."

Tabitha warned, "Who is going to stop them? You? You can barely walk. When you arrived we thought you had two broken arms. Look at your arms, they are still badly bruised." "What am I going to do Tabitha?"

Tabitha did not have an answer. "I don't know. I have been in this harem, almost all of my life. The Herders stole my mother. She gave birth to me out in the desert and concealed me for a long time. Some of the other concubines agreed to hide and take care of me. Mother taught me how to speak Latin. She said that it would help me escape someday. We often would speak to each other in Latin and so no one would understand us. About a year ago, Bara found out about me. Bara killed my mother but spared me. He said that I would be a strong worker and that it would only be a couple of years and I would make a good concubine.

"Mother was very old and could do little work in the fields. I think he killed her because she cost more to feed than she produced in the fields. I have to work in the fields like others, but they protect me from the heat. The women will not be as good to you because you are a threat to them. Stories about how Bara treated you have made all of them very angry. They compete for his attention. You will have to be careful." Barely speaking Magdala asked, "Tabitha, why are you being so kind to me, you don't even know me?" Tabitha gave her a warm look, "You remind me of my mother. She had light skin like yours and seemed to be from a far-away world, like you. While you were ill you mumbled in Latin about your home in Rome, something called Vestals, and someone named Augustus. You even sounded like my mother."

It took Magdala several more days to gain her strength. Every day or so Bara would come to the door of the tent and order Magdala into the fields. When he saw that she could not even rise up, he would hit her. With dark glaring eyes he said, "You better get well soon, or you will find yourself strapped to a pole in the sun." Magdala was stunned by the change in Bara. Where was the tender, loving, gentle man that she had known so intimately? He had become a violent slave driver who cared little for her or anyone else. Tabitha came to Magdala, "You don't understand, do you? "Understand what?" "Bara is a Herder, no more or less. He is Chief of the Tribes and has been Chief for as long as anyone can remember. If you disagree with him, he will kill you." Magdala disagreed, "I argued with him, but I am still alive?" Tabitha chided her, "You are lucky. I have seen him kill both Herders and women. He must care a little for you."

The nightmare continued for Magdala. How could this man seduce her? Tabitha was wise beyond her years, "Herders know how to gently seduce a woman through kindness. I am sure that Bara was kind to you.

Then when you give into their kindnesses they can no longer stand the sight of you. You are an animal in their eyes. They enjoy the punishment of that animal. As long as you don't give into their sexual advances, you are safe. Normally after the first sexual encounter a woman is severely beaten." And Magdala was beaten, but it came days after she was intimate with him. She thought that they shared so much together, but she was wrong. "Tabitha how is it that you know so much?" Tabitha answered, " I listen and watch. I know a lot."

The very next day Bara came to the tent and Magdala did not listen to Tabitha. She was feeling better and greeted him at the tent door. Immediately Bara struck out at her. "Bara," she exclaimed, "Stop hitting me with the whip." Bara was hitting her face and hands, tearing her flesh. "No woman speaks to me in public. You will never speak to me again unless I will it. Get out into the fields, it is time that you paid for your tent and food." Whimpering like a beaten animal, Magdala followed the other women to the fields. Tabitha pointed toward a huge grove of wild Cactus plants. "You must harvest their fruit." Tabitha thrust her hand into the Cactus plant and picked the sweet sabre. "See how easy it is. Be careful, the hairs of the Cactus will hurt you and cause your face and arms to swell."

Magdala thrust her hand into the Cactus toward the fruit. The stinging hairs of the plant stuck in her hand and arm. She screamed. Tabitha explained, "Leave them in your hand, you will never be able to pull them out. Within a few weeks your hands will be tough and you will not feel the prick. Be careful, too many of those needles could kill you." Tabitha peeled back the crusty layer of the fruit and inside was a delicious watery substance like a melon. This fruit kept the Herders alive. It was often their only source of water, of survival.

Meanwhile in Caesarea, Magdala and her caravan were long overdue. The Migration administrators feared the worst. Chusa was called and he relayed the bad news to Philip and his daughters. While they were sad at the loss of Magdala, they were in constant fear for their own lives. Romans were torturing Jews in the theatre. They had become sport for the aristocrats. Some said that they had planned a march of all the Jews down the main street of the city. Hastily, Philip and Chusa made plans to escape. Chusa knew of a secret retreat in the foothills of southern Judea. One night while the Roman guards at the city gates slept, they crawled on their hands and knees to the road to Jericho, the road to the south. By day they hid in the brush and at night they walked until the sun came up. Within a few days they had arrived at the retreat near Beersheba.

Magdala grew more tired and lost more weight due to working in the sun all day long. She was eating but the fevers were keeping her from sleeping at night. When she did fall asleep, it was only a matter of minutes before her nightmares would awake her, screaming. The other concubines kept their distance. They had seen it before, the fevers. No foreign woman had ever recovered from Fularia.

Long ago, Herders used to sleep with their goats and sheep. Many of the animals were infested with parasites. Some of the animals began to die. First they would lose weight, then their energy to walk, and finally they would sleep all day. You could see huge parasites roaming in their body under their skin. Finally all of the animals died. When they died the parasites would crawl out of their eyes and into someone or another animal. Even before an animal died, if they were wounded or cut, the parasites would crawl out of their bodies. Those parasites crawled into the ears, nose, mouth and other openings in the body and infected the Herders. Many died, but many also survived and carried the disease with them. Only Herders could survive the fevers. Bara had infected her with the disease when they made love. Each day Magdala grew weaker. The parasites had caused her to bleed constantly as if she was in her monthly courses. It would not stop. Tabitha knew that Magdala would have to find help or she would die. She began to plan Magdala's escape to a nearby town.

Sometimes at the end of a good harvest, the Herders would travel to Beersheba or Jerusalem to sell extra fruit. Often Bara would pick one of his favorite concubines to ride with him to market. "Magdala," said Tabitha, "You have to leave here. You will die if you do not find help. Tonight I will ask Bara if I can ride with him to market. He has been very nice to me lately and I think he wants me. If he says yes, then I will beg him to take you with us. Be ready at sundown."

Tabitha's plan worked. Bara was more than happy to take both of them with him to Jerusalem. His personality seemed to be totally different than it had during the past few weeks. On the way into the city they laughed and joked. Magadala seemed to be improving. When they finally arrived late in the night, Bara placed their mats under the wagon and he went to sleep in his own tent. Magdala cried, "Tabitha, how can he be so different. It has only been a few months since he promised to love and take care of me." "Magdala, he desires you and wants you to forget about his violent side. Herders are supposed to treat their concubines this way or they will have no respect or power over the other Herders."

"Magdala, we will escape while he is sleeping." Magdala was afraid, "He will hear us!" Tabitha assured her, "No, he will not. I have some special medicine for him." Underneath her robe, Tabitha pulled out a large dagger. "I found this in the sand the day the Centurions were murdered and you were brought back to camp. I was there, but you did not notice me." The dagger's handle was golden and on it was carved the golden sign of fire that resembled the emblem on Magdala's cheek. Magdala gasped, "Bara told me that the Centurions were being held at another village. What happened to them?" Tabitha told the sad story, "They were all killed or left to die in the desert without food or water. I snuck out into the desert to see what I could find. The Herders missed many things when they fought Bara for you."

Magdala began to sob as she grieved for all of those men. How could she have been so deceived by Bara? And as she looked up, Bara was standing over her. "Are both of you okay? I thought I heard a wild animal howling near you?" "No, there are no wild animals around here tonight Bara, but would you mind, if I came over to your tent for a little while," said Tabitha. Sweetly, Bara said, "My dear, you are always welcome in my tent."

Magdala was horrified as Tabitha followed Bara back to his tent. Why was she doing this? Within an hour, Tabitha ran back to Magdala with blood all over her face and clothing. She whispered to Magdala, "Hitch up the mules as quietly as you can, we have to leave right now before the others discover him." With hands dripping with blood, Tabitha drove the mules hard toward the lights of the city. Magdala watched for the Herders. They would escape only because of Tabitha's courage. As Tabitha lay next to Bara in the tent, he turned over to kiss her. At that moment, with both hands she thrust the knife into the side of his neck as she said, "This is for my mother and for all the years I have been your captive." Bara immediately grasped his neck as blood spurted everywhere. He lunged for Tabitha but she was too quick. The wound was so great that he could not speak and immediately lost consciousness.

The two ragged travelers made their way through the streets to the nearest Centurion's post. Magdala told her story to the Centurion at the gates to Antonia's Castle and they believed her. Within days she was placed on a horse bound for Caesarea. This time twenty Centurions guarded her. Magdala begged Tabitha to go with her. "I cannot come with you. I must find out if I have a family. I have to find my father if he is still alive. My mother used to tell me about our farm just outside of Jerusalem. The Romans have promised to help me. If I get into trouble or need your help, I will send a message."

Magdala hugged Tabitha and left her standing in front of the Centurion's post. She loved this brave little person. One of the administrators in Jerusalem had advanced Magdala some of her salary. She took it and placed it in Tabitha's hands. "This may help you." Tabitha warned, "Take care of yourself Magdala, find a healer as soon as possible." Magdala felt better. Clean water and clothing along with good food gave her strength. She still had the fevers but she was able to ride a horse. Perhaps the concubines were wrong.

When Magdala arrived in Caesarea, she headed straight for Chusa's wonderful old house, anticipating seeing Philip and his daughters. Certainly they believed she was dead. As she walked down the street leading to his house she could see burning timbers. Running to a neighbor's house, Magdala asked, "Have you seen Chusa? What happened to his house?" The neighbor hesitated, "Well, you know, everyone knows, he is dead. They are all dead!"

CHAPTER EIGHT
GALILEE
C.E. 25

"Galilee offered a splendid oasis for the unhealthy."

In the north, far from the street vendors and the excitement of Jerusalem was Galilee. From deep within the earth precious spring water bubbled up out of the springs of Dan and met the scorching sun. Desert sands as tall as mountains stopped on the eastern edge of the Sea that nourished Galilee. Its green valleys and hillsides invited the weary to rest, to revive, and to refresh.

From every village in the Empire people traveled to Galilee looking for answers to both problems of the body and the soul. If the hot sulfur baths did not help them then the cool breezes of the fresh spring or sea would soothe their anxieties. It was here in this beautiful tourist town of the north that the seeds for revolution were sown. On pebble-lined roads that led to the Sea of Galilee, Lysander lived the life of a person of the streets. Every day he held out his hands to the needy and every day someone was rescued from a disease or problem. Slowly, Lysander was becoming the hope for the lost, forsaken, unloved, and poor. They trusted him to reinvent their future.

Magdala's chest felt as if it would explode as she walked along the famous shores of the Sea of Galilee. She scanned the desert that made its way to the edge of the sea. She thought, "The desert will conquer the sea one day!" The sand seemed to weigh heavily upon Magdala's shoulders. It was inevitable, no matter how many Asclepioi or healers she had consulted, she was going to die. After finding Chusa's house destroyed and no trace of

Philip, she went on a journey to find someone to help her with the fularia. The healing waters of Dan could not help her. The hot springs increased her fevers. The mud baths suffocated her. There was no relief from the drenching heat that radiated from within her. She could feel the parasites growing. Most days she slept and could only raise her head to eat.

Back in Caesarea the Migration Administrators agreed that Magdala deserved a rest. The trauma she suffered in the desert, they thought, had brought a decline in her health. Even while fighting the fevers, Magdala was very good at her job, winning support from the Roman elite. They liked her style. Her ability to speak many languages put her in close proximity to the highest officials of the Empire. Its coastal breezes attracted many from Rome. She would translate for visiting dignitaries and was often called to sit by the side of the King of Judea when dealing with matters with foreigners. She was becoming an important asset to both the Roman administration and the local political officials in Caesarea. They did not want to lose her so they devised the plan to send her to Galilee. With encouragement from the Roman government, she was given six months leave with pay. They sent her to Galilee, to the healers, to find a cure for whatever was wrong with her.

When Magdala returned from the Dead Sea assignment after being abducted and beaten by Bara. She came home to nothing. She was devastated. She soon learned about the political situation. Apparently the city-folk in Caesarea had taken it upon themselves to punish the Jews who had refused to import and sell some of their goods. Things had gotten so bad that the Romans were dismissing any worker who had Jewish blood or was associated with a Jew. Hundreds of dedicated Roman workers, being suspect, were thrown out of their homes and forced to leave town. Even the Migration officer was refusing entrance to any more Jews.

While Chusa had served King Herod well by managing his estates in the south, his service did not stop the Romans from suspecting him or his neighbors from envying him. Many did not like to have a dark-skinned man as their superior or neighbor, especially if he was an aristocrat. According to the gossip, someone publicly accused Chusa of being Jewish. He was dismissed from his job while he was out of town. While riding back to Caesarea, some of the townspeople ambushed him shouting, "There's that Jew. There's that black man who has made so much money. There's Chusa. Let's get him."

Surprised by the assault, Chusa did not know what was happening. He thought he was being robbed. The mob knocked him off his horse and dragged him through the streets until it ended at his home. There, they threw him on the steps and lite his house on fire. His servants saw the torches and ran to Chusa, attempting to help him. People broke down doors and windows and took whatever they could from the house. The roof collapsed on some of them as the home burned. Underneath the stampeding feet of the mob, lay Chusa. To this day, the whereabouts of Chusa's body remains a mystery. Some say that the mob threw his body into the burning house.

On her own in this volatile city, Magdala found a room in an old rooming house run by a widow and went back to work. For three months she had visited every healer she could find. They all told her the same thing, that her disease was highly contagious and fatal. It was only found among the goats and Herders of the south. Magdala had walked the same route every day around the lake thinking about the end of her life. Day after day she poured out her heart to the sea and then went back to her lonely room to cry. Why did these things have to happen to her?

She regretted so many things. She should have died with the rest of the Vestals in Rome. And she had lost Philip and his daughters. Were they still alive somewhere in Judea? Nightly she dreamed of Bara beating her and imagined how Chusa was killed. She wished with all of her being that she had known her mother and father. She had no relatives to claim her body when she died. Despondent, afraid and alone, Magdala's disease began to break down her will to live.

One day, late in the evening, as she was finishing her walk around the sea, she noticed a great sand cloud coming up the hill. It was a crowd of people running after someone and shouting, "Lysander help me. Heal me! Make me happy! Feed me! Teach me the secrets of immortality. I want to live forever." Magdala climbed up the Synagogue steps to see what was going on. Watching the crowds come closer and closer, she remembered stories about Lysander raising the dead. Maybe he could heal her? She was willing to try anything now. As the crowd came closer to the temple, Magdala managed to inch her way toward the man they were following as he came toward the Synagogue. Hands were reaching out to him and he was trying to avoid all of them.

How she did it, she will never know. With all the energy she had left in her she thrust herself into the crowd toward Lysander and grabbed his coat as she fell to the ground. When she let go, something snapped inside her. She was filled with energy from the top of her head to her feet. Lysander, angrily, yelled, "Who touched me? And Magdala sheepishly said, "Me!" And for the moment, the disease left her. She was well. Lysander healed others that day but invited Magdala to have dinner with him at the home where he was staying. Of course, she accepted and walked with him down the long road to the edge of town. It was dark and the crowds had left. They began to talk.

Lysander never claimed that he healed her. He said that she had healed herself. She had the power; he did not consciously heal her. Lysander was a wonder man to Magdala. His magic was so strong that many went away claiming that he would be king some day. With his powers he could help the Empire, he could rule the world. Many gathered around him and begged that he would choose novices to teach. They wanted the powers of the Asclepioi too. He took many novices but most failed and went back to their homes.

His novices demonstrated great affection for him and disdain for sharing him with others, especially women. So when Lysander invited Magdala to join him, they spat upon her. "Go home and leave Lysander alone. You are not like us. What do you want with him? You cannot have him. You were healed, now go away. Get out of our sight!" But Lysander protected her from these insults. She was the only person in the world that did not try to manipulate or use him. She was healed, but she did not ask for personal favors like the others. She enjoyed him not what he could do for her. She treated him like a friend.

Most of the novices were farmers or fishers that had no formal education. None of them had ever experienced the lifestyles of the royalty or aristocrats. Consequently, they did not recognize Magdala's fine manners and abilities. Their crude world, similar to that of the Herders, did not value females. Nor could they value education or the cultures of others. Lysander recognized her worth and respected in much the same way that he had respected and loved Hygeia. Every day they spent together they became closer. Magdala felt his magnetic love and listened to him teach and watched him heal. Yet, down deep inside she was afraid. Was he really a man, a human being? How could he possess such powers?

Lysander began taking journeys with his novices. Some people in local towns opened their arms to all of them and supported their work but other townspeople threw rocks at them and forced them to leave. They were afraid of the powers and called him evil. None of the other novices ever spoke a word to Magdala except John the oldest son of Zebedee. They became friends immediately.

John was not happy running the family business and so when Lysander came to town offering a different kind of lifestyle, he joined him and never regretted it. He did not like the pressures of family life. His parents worried that he was getting older and had not taken a wife. They bought him wife after wife and concubine after concubine but John did not want them in his life. He did not want to be married and so, in a sense, he ran away from home to avoid the pressure to conform to their wishes. Confiding to Magdala, John admitted that he too shared a love for Lysander, a passionate love. Traveling with Lysander was the best place to be in all of Judea.

Magdala had been absent from her position for almost six months in Caesarea, when early one morning a courier awakened her. "Miss, I have been looking all over Galilee for you. I followed the trail of Lysander and found you. Some have said that there was a woman that looked like you with him. Here is a message for you. She opened the scroll, "Herod Antipas, Tetrarch of Galilee, requests your presence in Caesarea, immediately." The courier explained, "I was sent to find you and bring you back to Caesarea. Many of the Administrators feared that you were dead. I had almost given up when I heard stories of a woman following Lysander. Will you return with me."? Magdala was ecstatic, "Oh, yes, I will come with you. Please rest while I pack my things."

For some reason Magdala had forgotten about her job and life in Caesarea. With her new health, she had been engrossed in the journey with Lysander. Lysander did not want her to leave but she knew she had to leave. She could not go on begging like they did and she had no real powers to help anyone. She needed a job and she had to take care of herself. Saying farewell was not easy for her. To both Lysander and John she said, "I will be back some day."

Within hours of arriving in Caesarea Magdala was taken to the high court presided over by Herod. "Magdala, have you been in any revolutionary activities lately? Magdala answered sternly, "No, your Excellency, and I don't know what you mean by revolutionary?" "Have you had any contact withe people in Rome or the Senate? "No," responded Magdala. "As you know, I have been very ill and spent many months searching for someone who could help me. In my search, I met no one from Rome." Herod did not believe her. "My dear, this is very odd. I hold in my hands a letter from a relative of the late Emperor with the official seal of Augustus. Under authority of the Senate, this person has requested your presence in Rome. Do you know anyone in Rome?"

Magdala lied, "No, Sir!" He continued, "With the letter came a courier bringing 100,000 drachma. According to the letter, you must book passage on a ship for Rome. There the party who has written the letter will contact you at the house near the Great Temple. Extra money has been sent to pay for Centurions to guard you until you reach the temple. The money is yours if you make the trip to Rome, otherwise it will be returned to the owner." One hundred thousand drachmas, well, Magdala had never even seen that much money in her life. Only a tiny portion of the money would be needed for the trip. The rest would be left with the Treasury in Caesarea. She looked to the King. She did not know what to do? Was it safe? Did he know the person who sent the letter? "Do you have any suggestions for me?" The King answered, "No, the decision is yours. Two men and a woman will be assigned to travel with you. The seas are calm this time of year and so the ship should be safe. If you left within the week, you could return before the winter storms."

Magdala had nothing to lose and so agreed to the terms of the letter. For the next week she visited almost every shop in Caesarea buying clothing and supplies for her trip. She was, at last, healthy and happy and anticipating a better future than her past. On the morning she was to sail, thee people were sent to her. Outside her cabin door stood two Centurions. They told her that a personal servant was already inside the cabin. And there sitting on the bed was Tabitha. "What are you doing here, Tabitha? Are you a passenger on the ship too? Where have you been? Did you find your father? Tabitha grabbed Magdala and hugged her.

"It is so good to see you, Magdala," said Tabitha. "I will tell you everything, everything soon." Magdala observed that the child had grown and looked healthier. "Magdala, I have taken a new name. I am called Dorcas now and believe it or not, I have been assigned to take care of you on this trip." It was too good to be true. Fate had brought them together again. Like old friends, they talked about their adventures in the desert and the cure Magdala experienced, even the mysterious letter.

Dorcas did not fare as well as Magdala. Having searched and questioned many people about her mother and father, she finally found an old woman Anna who remembered them. She told Dorcas this story, "Sackaria, your father, and your mother Isabel were up in years when you were born. You were a twin. Your brother's name was Vanya. Both of you brought such happiness to your parents. One day while your mother was working in the fields with your father, the Herders came and left your father for dead, while stealing your mother and the twins. Your father recovered and began looking for his family. He sold his farm and spent his days in the desert. They say that he died of a broken heart but I really don't know what happened to him." Dorcas did not know that she had a brother. No one had ever told her about him. She wondered what happened to him too. She also wondered why she had been told that she was the only child of her mother.

"I went back to the Roman official near Beersheba and asked him to help me find my father but he was unsuccessful. He knew that I was alone and had discovered that my brother lived in the desert somewhere. He offered me a job and I took it. He changed my name to Dorcas. I was a servant and he liked my work so well that he recommended me for a position in the house of Herod. Herod liked my work so well that he assigned me to work with you. It is my holiday too!" Magdala was very happy to see Dorcas but also sad that she could not find her father. "Look at you, you have survived everything! Your parents would be so proud of you."

And it was a good holiday for both of them. The ship left Caesarea and within a week docked at Corinth on the Aegean Sea. Here they spent a few days while the captain and crew readied the ship to travel overland. Sailing around the tip of Achaia could prove fatal if the winds changed. Many ships had broken apart on the reefs that jutted out into the Mediterranean. At Corinth ships could cross over to the Adriatic without risking the reefs. The ship was hoisted up out of the water onto a gigantic wagon that was pulled across the land and then deposited in the Adriatic. It was a colossal feat but it saved a lot of ships and lives.

High above the city of Corinth rose the Acrocorinth. Military personnel watched over this city day and night while stationed on top of this mountain. You could see a hundred miles on a clear day. In the shadow of this natural protection, Corinth prospered. The road to the East went through the heart of the city. Almost everyone who traveled from East to West stopped in Corinth. Greeting the travelers were at least ten thousand sacred prostitutes. Worshipping at one of the temples in town was a huge tourist attraction. While Magdala and Dorcas enjoyed and indulged themselves in the public baths and sanctuaries of the Gods and Goddesses, the captain of the ship reported that there would be a delay. The front section of the hull of the ship had collapsed when they began to release it from the pulley on the wagon, they would have to stay in Corinth for a few more weeks before they continued their journey.

Magdala and Dorcas took advantage of the extra time in Corinth. One priestess suggested to them that the visit the Oracle at Delphi, quite a few miles to the west of Corinth. It would take about a day to sail there or a week by a caravan. Since the two had some time to enjoy Achaia, they boarded a small ship to Delphi. It only took them about a day to reach the port that was about twenty miles from the Oracle. High above the sea, on the hills to the north, they could see lights. It was a dazzling sight. The trek to the Oracle was going to take them a couple of days because the walk was up a mountain path. They stayed over night in the port and then began the trek with the rise of the early sun.

Both Magdala and Dorcas felt as if someone was following them as they trudged up the hill but they did not see anyone. They walked faster. For the people of Macedonia and Achaia, the Oracle of Delphi was at the center of the earth. It was here, only here, that the Gods communicated with people. You could hear them or least you could hear sounds that whistled and grumbled through the jagged mountains that rose six thousand feet above sea level. Priests, after taking payment, would interpret these sounds for visitors and seekers. And it was through the Pythia that the Gods spoke the loudest.

The Oracle at Delphi was a mouthpiece for the God, Apollo and all the power in the heavens. People traveled to Delphi from all over the world to seek advice from the priests of Apollo. Their answers came through the mumblings of a virgin called Pythia. Each year the priests would search the villages through the tribes of Macedonia and Achaia for a woman who would be dedicated to the Gods. Several times a year young virgins would be brought to the lower floor of the Temple of Apollo. There they would be given mysterious potions and placed upon a tripod sitting over a crack in the foundation of the temple. With incantations, smoke, and libations the Pythia would breathe the fumes that would come out of the crack in the floor. Many people thought that the temple was built on top of a volcano. Years later an earthquake would destroy almost everything on this mountaintop.

The ritual of the Pythia included potions and herbs given to her by the priests. In her trembling stupor she would utter syllables. Those syllables were interpreted by the priests of Apollo as messages from their God. Each syllable was copied and then interpreted for the seeker. Of course, all of this work was done for a huge fee. The priests of Apollo at the Oracle claimed that they could find out the answer to any question. But the only people who received the answers were the ones who could afford their services.

For those unfortunate who did not have the sufficient resources to request an oracle from Apollo, there were lesser Gods and Goddesses willing to take their money. Athena, the virgin Goddess of intelligence, who bravely watched over Athens in the Acropolis, was relegated here to a small temple at the foot of the hill. Here her priestesses also interpreted oracles for a price. All along the causeway up the hill towards the great Temple of Apollo, lesser Gods and Goddesses offered their advice to travelers. Visiting the Oracle at Delphi was unlike any other place on earth. While waiting for an answer from a priest or priestess, seekers could indulge themselves with pleasure and excitement. High on top of the mountain was a hippodrome where chariot races and other competitive sports took place daily. About half way up the mountain, carved deep into its side was an open-air theatre where statesmen spoke and players challenged visitors to think about the role of the Gods and Goddesses in their lives.

Magdala came to the oracle to find out about her future and her past. Willing to pay the asking price of one of the priests of Apollo, she was taken into the inner sanctuary immediately. One priest spoke, "Woman, do you understand that we do not control Apollo? We are only interpreters. What we hear is not under our control. "Yes, I understand," said Magdala. "Do you promise to accept our message whether it be for good or evil?" Magdala nodded her head as a yes.

She stepped behind Dorcas to get out of the way of the young and beautiful Pythia who sat in the midst of glowing candles and smoke. One of the priests gave her something to drink and eat. She was chewing on something. As she sat upon a tripod, she began to twist and turn. A great rumble shook the temple as hot air and smoke rose out of the hole in the floor. The woman began to moan and then fell on the floor. Magdala ran to help her but was stopped by two armed guards. "You cannot interfere," yelled the High priest," This is the way Apollo wills it to be done. "The woman is dying," gasped Magdala, "we must help her." Magdala had no idea that her questions would cause such harm to another person. As the woman moaned, the priests copied down her sounds and interpreted them for Magdala. The High Priest handed her a note that read, "If you search, you will find. If you find, you will change. If you change, you will search. If you search, you will find. When you find, the end will have a beginning."

Both Magdala and Dorcas read the poem that was in Greek and asked, "What does this mean?" "It means what it says. The meaning is in the words. It will happen exactly as we have written, " said the High Priest. Magdala did not believe the High Priest. "You have taken all of my money for this?" The High Priest warned her, "Beware and do not curse Apollo or his priests. It is time for you to leave." Magdala pondered the last phrase, "The end will have a beginning" which had no meaning for her. But it soon would mean everything. She was about to embark on the most challenging and dangerous mission in her life. Rome waited for her anxiously.

The journey back to Corinth took no time. The ship had been fixed and so they were off to Rome. When they arrived at the port south of Rome, Ostia, Magdala decided to visit Philip's farm before proceeding to the city. The Centurions protested but gave into her wishes. Renting a wagon at the port, all of them headed toward Philip's old home. But it was

Magdala's home too. Memories began to flood her brain and tears sprang into her eyes. Oh how she missed Philip and his daughters. Arriving at the house, they saw smoke billowing out its huge chimney.

The wagon stopped at the gate. Magdala did not know what to do. An old man came out of the house, "What do you want?" Magdala took a second look, her mind must have been playing tricks on her, because he sounded like Philip. Stepping up into the wagon, the man spoke again, "What do you want, if you want something say it loud and clear." Magdala was right, it was Philip. He was alive. Tears rolled down her eyes again. "Philip, Philip, it is me Magdala!" The old man did not recognize her and pushed her away. "Who are you? Go away, go away!" bellowed the old man. Someone came to the door and shouted, "Magdala, where on earth? Come in, come into the house!"

Philip's illness had taken its toll on the man; he did not even recognize his own children any longer. In spite of his loss of memory, they were all happy to have found each other. Magdala introduced Dorcas and the Centurions and told them about her mission to Rome. All evening they traded stories about their adventures. After dinner they sat around the fire. The daughters relived their anguish in Judea by retelling the horrid story about their flight and escape from Caesarea. Hiding in the hills, they secretly waited for Chusa to bring supplies so that they could travel overland and find new home for themselves in Asia. To their horror, Chusa was killed the very night they were supposed to leave. The daughters blamed themselves for his death. Many of the Roman officials had been watching him because of his religious practices. Without supplies and money, they could not leave the country. Fortunately about a month after his death, they managed to stow away on a ship bound for Rome. No one detected them on the ship. They lived on the ship at night foraging for food and hid during the day. They never wanted to leave their home again.

Soon it was time to leave. It was getting late and all of the travelers had to get to Rome before the city gates closed. Promising to return, they left for the great city. Following directions through the streets and alleys of Rome, Magdala easily found the house next to the Great Temple. With her heart pounding so loud she could hardly speak, Magdala knocked on the huge door. A small young woman came to the door, "Hello, I am Magdala. I have been sent to talk with someone in this house. The servant went back into the house and then returned. "My mistress knows nothing of Magdala. If you want something to eat go around to the back of the house. She knows nothing about you and will not see you." Magdala tried to explain, "We are not beggars. I have an official letter from," and the door slammed in her face.

CHAPTER NINE
INHERITING THE PAST

"The old woman chuckled at the irony."

Ominous shadows clung to her every footstep as she etched her way down vacant alleys toward the arena. Tightly clutching her cloak wrapped around the stained parchment, Magdala could not imagine what lay ahead of her. She had waited. And with each moment she began to doubt the existence of her benefactor. One of her friends at the Migration office had surely played a trick on her. It was settled, she and Dorcas would return to Judea tomorrow.

On the eve of their departure, Magdala was jolted out of bed by an enormous thud at her villa door. Just as the pounding stopped a parchment edged its way slowly through a crack. Creeping very close to it as she carried her oil lamp, Magdala could see that it was covered with a stain. On the outer flap was the stamp of the Emperor, not just any Emperor. It was the sign of her beloved deceased uncle. Gasping for breath, Magdala read the words inside, "Meet my servant next to the coliseum doors facing the Forum in one hour. Come alone or not at all." "Are you okay Magdala? I heard a loud noise and for some reason I thought something had happened to you," cried Dorcas. Thrusting the scroll behind her, Magdala calmly said, "No, I am okay. I could not sleep." Dorcas explained, "I must have been dreaming, sorry to bother you. Are you sure you did not hear anything outside your door? I could have sworn I heard a legion of gladiators out there?"

"Something woke me too! I don't know what? Go back to sleep. Don't worry, I am fine," replied Magdala. Bewildered, Dorcas headed toward her room, intending to return. In an instant, Magdala threw on a cape and headed for the Coliseum. Rome was a very dangerous place after dark and Magdala knew the risks. Once she thought she heard someone behind her, but could not see anyone. She quietly crept along the way with only the moon for light, so she thought.

Just before the sun could poke its head up on the horizon, a bedraggled and exhausted Magdala reached the southern doors of the Coliseum. There was no one in sight. Looking through the crack in the doors, she could see that the floor of the Coliseum was gone. There were burned floating ships in water that filled the bottom of the Coliseum. Magdala wondered how many sailors had lost their lives in the mock naval battle. Rome liked its sport, the bloodier the better. If none of the combatants in the staged drama fell by the sword, the audience would choose who would die.

"Magdala!" a voice rang out. Startled, Magdala turned toward the voice she could not see. "Magdala," whispered a short stocky woman. "Follow me!" On the other side of the Coliseum a cart and driver waited for them. Together they galloped through the early morning until they reached the rolling hills outside of Rome. Hiding the cart, they began climbing up a very narrow winding path of a mountain that seemed to have no end. Magdala could not see her feet as she climbed the rocks. The old woman would reveal nothing to her. Finally on solid, flat ground, the woman took Magdala by the hand through an entrance to a cave. As they walked deeper and deeper into the mountain, Magdala felt as if she was being swallowed alive. What was at the end of the passageway? What would she find?

The walkway began to widen. Blocking their way were huge carved doors. Walking through the doorway made Magdala feel as if she were a little girl again going to visit the Emperor. White marble ceilings and walls greeted their eyes while their feet sunk deep into a thick blue carpet. Over to one side of the enormous room was a small bed and chair. Motioning with her hand, the woman offered Magdala a chair and something to eat. "Please explain to me what is going on and why am I here?" asked Magdala. "Magdala, thank you for trusting me. They call me, Tess. I am Cassia's personal servant. She will speak to you in the morning. This will be your room for the remainder of your time with us." Magdala did not like her explanation. "This huge room is big enough for a hundred people. What am I here and why are you leaving me alone?" Tess would not answer.

Magdala could not believe her eyes. They had traveled for hours away from the city high in the mountains, yet this cave was cleaner and exquisitely furnished. "Tess, who is Cassia and why does she want to see me?" There was no answer. Magdala began to worry. She had not told Dorcas or the Centurions where she was going. Was she mad? Maybe these people had discovered that she was the only one to survive the sacrifice of the Vestals. Were they going to punish her cowardice so long ago? Had she walked into a trap?

Tess could see that Magdala was exhausted from her trip. "I will answer your questions tomorrow. Please rest for now," said Tess as she slipped out of the huge wooden doors, locking them as she went. Hours later, still wearing her dirty cape, Magdala was awakened by Tess. "Your bath is poured and clean clothes are lying next to your bed on the chair. I will return with your breakfast in about an hour."

Magdala enjoyed the bath and the breakfast but she was so frightened that her hands trembled. She had to find out who sent for her and why? Tess returned and led her down another long and huge hallway that seemed to link two passageways. At the end of the causeway stood immense jade gates. Guards motioned for them to pass. Entering another marble room even more ornately carved than the first, Magdala could see someone sitting at the end of a long black table. The closer she came; she could see that the figure was a woman. The woman stood up and slowly walked toward them. Reaching for Magdala, she grabbed her arm with one hand and took hold of her cheek with the other. Magdala could only imagine the worst. "You have the sign of the Vestal on your cheek. You are indeed Magdala. I was worried that you had erased the scar. Welcome, I am Cassia and I sent for you." Staring at the woman and unable to speak, Magdala's eyes darted over to a young man sitting in a stuffed chair to the side of the table. He was about her age and his posture was alert and stiff. Their eyes met for an instant, remembering Bara, Magdala instantly looked away.

Finely braided long dark hair covered the shoulders of the old woman. Magdala could see golden pins holding back the sides of her hair. On her neck hung a necklace filled with all sorts of jewels. She had been a beautiful woman, earlier in her life. Time had erased the sparkle and vitality of youth. Like a servant before royalty, Magdala humbly sat. The older woman spoke, "Come sit with us. I know you must be very puzzled and frightened. You do not need to be afraid of us. You can trust us." I am Cassia and this is my son Judas Didymus. We are so happy that we found you. We have been looking for you for years.

And so they told their story to Magdala. Augustus had taken Cassia as his lover in his early twenties. She was the only woman that he ever really loved. To prove his love for her he built the marble palace in the mountains for her. It was her underground castle. This is where Augustus came when he wanted to escape politics and family. Secretly, he had spent millions on the construction. Virtually no one in Rome knew about this place because he used foreign workers and took great precautions to hide it from everyone. It was built with his own money. Some of the Herders in the area knew about the building but did not pay much attention to it. Shrines to Gods and Goddesses were built all over the countryside. They figured it was just another one of those religions that had a secret underground room where they worshipped. Sometimes an occasional traveler took refuge in the stone entrance but no one had ever discovered the passageway into the castle.

Guards had been assigned by Augustus, watched all of the passageways to the entrances day and night. They had stayed to help Cassia after Augustus had died because she paid them so well. As Magdala listened, she grew impatient with their story. "What does all of this have to do with me? It is very interesting but ...." Cassia responded with equal vigor, "Magdala, you are the child of a Queen of Egypt and the brother of Augustus. If Augustus had not executed his brother, he would have been heir to the throne. "I am a relative of Augustus?" said a bewildered Magdala. "Yes, you are his niece and only days before he died, he rewrote his will leaving you millions of drachma."

Magdala was stunned. All of those years with Philip and living day to day with hardly enough food came rushing into her mind. She was an heiress and she did not know it. "How do you know so much about Augustus' will? And why are you interested in his wishes," quipped Magdala. Judas intervened, "My mother was mentioned at the reading of the will. Augustus left her over a quarter of his estate. Up until now, we have not needed any of that money because Augustus had his own personal Treasury in the mountains. But it has been almost twenty years since his death and the money is running low. My mother is getting older and will need more assistance. I do not want her to have to live like a commoner. We need to prove that she has claim to the estate. When her name was read, it shocked all of the relatives. They were embarrassed that so much of his estate would be left to a common concubine. Mother was not present at the reading of the will. After a few months the will was placed in the Treasury at the Great Temple of the Vestals. It has been sitting in the inner sanctuary since that day. Mother found out about the reading from a friend of hers who was in the Senate. But it was too late; no one would listen to her. We have tried to persuade the Roman officials that we have a claim on the estate of Augustus. No one will believe us. They would not even look at the will in the Temple."

Ignoring Judas, Magdala exclaimed, "Didn't they look for me after the burning of the Vestals?" Yes," continued Cassia, they could not find your remains in the temple. They reasoned that because you were so small that you may have been lost in the rubble. You know, don't you, that the High Priest was sentenced to death for his outrageous act. No one understood why he did it. The laws provide for punishment but not wholesale slaughter. Before they could execute him, he escaped. No one has heard from him since that time. Some say that he killed himself."

Magdala was ecstatic! All of those years she thought that it was her fault that the Vestals were burned. Did she cause their deaths? In her child's memory, she thought that she was actually responsible for their deaths. She always feared that someone would find out what she had done. "If we are to inherit all of this fortune, how do we prove that we are heirs to the throne," asked Magdala. Cassia answered, "Stored away in the vault guarded by the Vestals is a will that is handwritten and stamped with the seal of Augustus. This document was verified by the mark of the Vestals on the day it was deposited into the temple." "But the temple was burned to the ground, " stammered Magdala.

"While the Great Temple was razed, the Treasury was placed within a solid rock structure underground. All of the documents, jewels, furniture, and gold were untouched by the fire," explained Cassia. "Augustus told me about this document only days before he died. I tried to send someone to retrieve it but it was on the same day the Vestals were burned. No one was allowed near its ruins and the Treasury below. And since Augustus is dead, I can no longer use his signet ring," as she pointed to her finger.

"I made a promise to Augustus on his death bed that when he died I would no longer use his name on documents and that I would take care of you, Magdala, for the rest of your life. It was only by accident that I found you in Caesarea working in the Migration office. I could not be sure of your identity until I met you personally and saw the mark of the Vestals. Judas has agreed to help recover the document. And has worked on a plan of how to enter the temple." Magdala looked at Judas, "Why would you risk your life for me? What do you expect to gain from all of this?" Judas answered, "I want to help my mother. She has no family, other than myself, and no place to go."

As the morning wore on, Judas and Magdala seemed to enjoy each other more and more. Together they studied the plans of the temple. It was reconstructed according to the original design. Magdala's memory helped to underscore a plan for finding and opening the Treasury. By the end of the second day, Magdala and Judas knew that they would need a third person. But who would that be? Magdala persuaded them to trust

Dorcas.

During the next week while they devised a plan to recover Augustus' will, Magdala would often catch Judas gazing at her. "How long have you lived inside this mountain?" asked Magdala. "All of my life and then some" retorted Judas. "My life is reasonable. Now since I am older, I can come and go as I please from this castle. But when I was younger, it was very lonely. Mother would never allow me to go to the city. She was afraid that people would find out about her hideaway and take it away from us. I had foreign tutors who taught me how compute and to write. I even learned how to ride a horse and defend myself. Yet, I was alone as a child. I did not have any friends that were my age. I was just thinking, if I had known you when I was a child, I would have made you my friend."

Magdala blushed as she continued the conversation, "Why it is as if you have no past. What do you tell people when you meet them in the city?" Judas answered, "I tell them that I am from Gaul." Magdala asked him if he had learned a trade where he could make money. "I am well-educated and could certainly serve Rome in some way, but I have never had a job. Mother wanted me to know what it was like to live like royalty. The only problem is that without her inheritance, I cannot continue to live this way."

Magdala and Judas talked on and on, each passing moment brought them closer and closer. On the way to the city to find Dorcas they laughed and played like children. Somehow the gravity of their mission did not frighten them. It was a game, a child's game. Dorcas was astonished to see Magdala and her escort. "Where have you been? I thought you had been abducted or killed. Where did you go the other night? We have missed our ship to Caesarea!" Magdala tried to calm Dorcas, "I have much to explain to you. Come, meet Judas. He is a friend of mine."

Hours later they all sat together planning their assault on the temple. Dorcas agreed to help Magdala if she would share her fortune with her. Fifty thousand drachmas seemed a fair price. They waited for night to fall before they proceeded to the temple. As they approached the temple, their plans seemed frail compared to the thick temple walls and its imposing gates. While many people had access to its outer sanctuary only Vestals were allowed to venture down the narrow underground path to the Treasury. From the inner sanctuary it went down at least one hundred feet, around and around until the opening became so small that only one person could enter. The only light on this entrance was a Vestal who was on duty in the Treasury room on the other side of the wall. Small slips of light shone through cracks in the wall. Finally the last step was a metal door barred by a huge stone pin.

Since the founding of the Temple of Vesta, hundreds of years ago, Vestals changed watch over the Treasury every six hours. No outsider had ever penetrated all of the doors and passed by all of the guards who watched over the Vestals. It was an impossible journey. Yet, Magdala remembered an entrance into the temple that had long been forgotten. Together the threesome walked out into the country to find the small cave that saved Magdala's life so many years ago. It would not be an easy find. But Magdala had a good memory and just before nightfall they found a small hole in the field near the road that led to the city. Lighting their torches they entered the dark causeway.

For hours they crawled and sometimes walked the underground path, never knowing whether or not they had chosen the correct path. Dorcas was worried, "Are you sure that this leads to the Temple?" "It did many years ago," answered Magdala. "I hope that we are going in the right direction." A small stream trickled slowly along the floor of the cave. All of the adventurers were like animals crawling on all fours. And as they crawled, the opening became smaller and smaller. "I don't remember the cave being this small," remarked Magdala. Judas understood the problem, "You were only a child. You have a child's memory of this passage." Dorcas moaned, "I hope we make it out of here alive."

Soon they were crawling on their stomachs. They placed their bags on their back because they were becoming soaked. "Ahh," screamed Judas, "I hit my head on the cave ceiling. I think that the cave ends here. There is no place to go." Magdala rubbed his head. "Let me see if I can find an opening." Magdala took a rock and began pounding on the walls to determine if there was a passageway. Judas was concerned, "Won't they hear us inside? Do you think you should be doing this? Magdala finished hitting the walls and thought that they had reached the end of the journey. Dorcas backed up and tried to stretch out her legs and sit down, when suddenly a rock gave way beneath her feet. "Magdala, here's something. There is a small passageway that goes down and then up again. Could this be the place?" Magdala thought that maybe their luck had turned, "I don't know. It was so long ago and everything seems so different. Let's try it."

One by one they slithered up the dark passageway. It was so small that they could not bring torches. At one point Judas was caught between two huge boulders but managed to wiggle out. Magdala led the way. The game they were playing yesterday was long gone and this game was not as much fun. She was tired and thirsty and wanted to stop but she kept crawling. After about an hour of crawling they reached the end of the passageway again. There was no sign of an opening. They must have plastered it when the Temple was rebuilt after the burning of the Vestals. Was all of this for nothing? "Shhh, quiet, I hear something. Listen," said Magdala, "I hear voices." Muffled sounds could be heard through the rocks. The voices seemed to be coming from below them. Could someone else be in the cave? Who would know about this old entrance?

Quietly they listened but could not understand a word that was spoken. The voices seemed to move from one place to the other. Unknown to the three they had crawled beyond the place where Magdala had escaped so long ago. The entrance to the inner sanctuary was far below them. "Those voices are not in the cave, " said Magdala. "They are coming from inside the Temple. Let's move back down the tunnel and push all around as we go down. Maybe the entrance is this way." Judas and Dorcas groaned. Their legs seem to turn to rubber. They had little strength left. Climbing up this old passageway was more difficult than crawling in the cave. Dorcas kept pushing the side of the cave with her feet. "It's no use, we will never get inside." Magdala pushed and listened and finally when they had almost reached the entrance to the passageway, they found a loose rock. "I think I have found it. Quiet, let me see if I can move it," whispered Magdala.

Sure enough, she had found a hole but as she moved the stone she realized that the opening was much too small for any of them to go through. "We will have to dig around this rock. Dorcas, listen for voices and Judas and I will try to dig around the opening." All of them had brought knives just in case they needed to protect themselves. The rock was set in thick plaster. Slowly they used their weapons to chop away at it until the hole was large enough for them to enter. They could see nothing as they began to climb again. A huge velvet curtain now hung on the walls of the inner sanctuary. As they climbed the curtain muffled their sounds. No one heard them enter.

One by one they crawled out of the hole and found themselves standing behind a curtain. They could hear voices but could not distinguish from which direction they were coming. "Magdala, which way now?" asked Judas. "Follow me, I think it is down this way." So down they went until they reached the end of the curtain. Judas was again pointing out the problems, "There is no light here. How do we know that there aren't guards around the next corner? " Magdala answered, "We don't, I only remember there being one Vestal at the door. It could have changed." They could see a flickering light as they quietly walked down the stairs. It was if they were walking into an abyss of the Nethers. "Dorcas, put on your dress," whispered Magdala. "Okay, but this seems a little silly. I don't even look like a Vestal. Look at my hands, do these hands look like the hands of royalty?" retorted Dorcas. "Okay," whispered Magdala, "there is the Vestal. Go on Dorcas. Remember not to say too much because your accent is so different from the people who live in Rome."

Quietly Dorcas stepped down toward the Treasury door. She was trembling inside but she did not show it. She had learned long ago never to show emotion when she was afraid. Many times it had kept her alive out in the desert. "Sister, I have come to replace you for the next few hours," said Dorcas. "I only arrived a few minutes ago. There must be some mistake. Go talk with the Priestess, she will straighten this out." " I can't," said Dorcas, "would you?" "You can't? What do you mean? Who are you anyway? You don't look like anyone I know?"

Quickly Magdala and Judas swooped down on the Vestal. She did not know what had hit her. Tied up, blindfolded, and gagged with items they had found in the passageway, they placed her in the corner next to the Treasury door. The large bolt was so heavy that it took both of them to lift it up. Neither of them noticed the secret rope that lay across the entrance. Magdala had never seen this room. "It's beautiful! I have never seen so many jewels and gold coins!" exclaimed Magdala.

On the wall were rows and rows of golden goblets and other items stamped with the state insignia. In the back were large jars filled with scrolls with more baskets of coins and gold nuggets. Elaborately carved furniture was stacked to the ceiling. "Magdala, do you have any idea where the will would have been filed," asked Judas. "No, what we will have to do is look for the seal of Augustus. There must be thousands of scrolls here, how will we ever find it?" Magdala ordered, "Let's just start looking. Dorcas watch the door while we look!"

Hours later left them empty-handed. They thought it would be with the other scrolls in the large jars. Judas kept forgetting the task at hand and began opening up boxes and touching the gold jewelry. Magdala had to scold him to keep him looking for the will. His eyes seemed to glow as he touched all of the wealth. Suddenly Judas screamed. His snooping had paid off! "Magdala, I've got it. Look it is in the blue sapphire chest over here with the furniture." Buried beneath furniture from around the globe, probably gifts to Augustus, was the scroll. It was wrapped in a Persian rug. "See, it has the seal of Augustus." It did have the seal. Magdala broke it and began to read. Dorcas warned, "Magdala, I hear voices. We must hurry. I think the Vestals are coming."

In their haste to leave the Treasury, Magdala and Judas tripped over the rope. Judas was carrying a huge bag of jewels. Magdala scolded, "What are you doing? Stealing was not part of the deal." Judas argued back, "They will never miss it and besides they owe it to me." There was no time to argue with Judas. They had to find their way out of the temple and fast. Quickly they shut the door to the Treasury locking the Vestal inside and quietly leaped up the stairs behind the curtains. They could not run fast enough from the approaching voices. Just as they reached the top of the stairs the great wooden doors swung open. The alarm had been sounded but services muffled the sound. Only a few rushed toward the Treasury.

Magdala and Judas hid behind the great curtain near the opening to the outside world. Catching their breath, they slipped through the space in the floor and made their way out into the field. "I do hope that Dorcas is safe. If our plan works she will be waiting for us at your mother's estate."

Meanwhile, Dorcas stood at the Treasury door. Several Vestals and not a few priestesses came toward Dorcas. She stood her ground. "What's the matter," said Dorcas. "What is going on? Has something happened upstairs?" Some of them said, "The alarm was sounded. Did you see anyone down here?" Dorcas replied, "No one new has passed this way. Where would they go?" Someone in the crowd said, "The bells rang and we thought that someone had broken into the Treasury." "See for yourself, open the doors and check. You will find nothing missing," chirped Dorcas hoping her Latin accent would not give her away.

The crowd took a step backward. None of them wanted to enter the Treasury. While most of them had stood guard at the Treasury, none of them had actually entered it. It was forbidden by orders of the high priest. It was said that those who entered without the blessing of Vesta would die instantly.

"Well, I am tired," said Dorcas, "Would one of you take my place for a couple of hours?" So Dorcas, hands hidden with a hood over most of her face, made her way up through all of the Vestals and step by step out into the courtyard that surrounded the temple. It was night, and to her amazement no one questioned her as she walked alone. When the guards were taking a break for supper, she sneaked into a doorway and quietly opened a door. Tearing off her Vestal garb, she ran for the mountains. She was safe and hoped that her partners were also. By the next morning all three were reunited at the base of the mountain retreat. Climbing the long single file walkway to the top was difficult for all of them. They had eaten and drank little during the day. Dorcas and Magdala were very tired and Judas could hardly carry his bag full of precious jewels and gold. At the top of the stairs were servants who brought them something to eat and drink, greeted them. Magdala sat down and took out the scroll and began to read.

"On this day under the watchful eye of Juno, I bequeath all of my belongings to those whom I love. To my wife, Livia, and her children Drusus and Tiberias, and my child Julia, I leave half of all of my estate. They shall inherit all of my properties in foreign countries and the house in the city. The rest of my fortune shall be divided amongst three people whom I have wronged most of my life. To Cassia, my lover and friend for over twenty years, I leave two million drachma, or at least one-sixth of everything I own. Long ago I promised the priests of Zeus that I would sacrifice a child to be born to my brother and his Egyptian lover. I could never do it. I took that child and its twin and gave it to Cassia to raise as her own. To this child called Judas Didymus (the twin) and his sister Magdala both born outside of the official marriage of my brother I leave the rest of my fortune. It should amount to four million drachma or one third of my estate. May Zeus forgive me for all whom I have wronged in my life. Sealed with the holy seal of Zeus himself, The Emperor Augustus Caesar."

Magdala kept reading the words over and over. She could hardly speak. "Judas, you are, you are ... my brother. Here, take the scroll and read it." At that very moment Cassia walked into the room. Pleased with their success, she asked for the scroll. She also could not believe her eyes. The Emperor had promised her that he would never tell anyone about Judas. Judas was a gift to her. She could never have children of her own. Cassia had welcomed the child into her lonely life on the mountain.

They all sat and looked at each other. What a surprise! No wonder Judas looked familiar and felt like family. Judas had Magdala's eyes and hair; even their hands were the same. Both were about the same height and build. Magdala was slightly thinner and had more of a chin than Judas. They were brother and sister, why could they have not seen it before? Cassia broke the silence, "Tomorrow, we will take this will to a Senator in the city. He has been a friend of mine for a long time, and one of the few people who knew about my life with the Emperor. He will help us!"

Early the next morning they all set out for the city. Cassia was dressed like a queen and was carried in a seat high above the crowd. People thought that she was a visiting dignitary or mistress of a king from a far away land. She was dignified and beautiful. She could have been an Empress. Entering the Senate building, the Curia were assembled. Cassia, talked with her friend. None of the three knew to whom she had spoken. She assured them that they did not need to know his name. To tell them his name would jeopardize his position in the government. On the next morning, the will was put on the agenda and read before the entire Senate. Cassia, Magdala, Dorcas, and Judas sat in the balcony waiting for their turn to testify.

Cassia explained to them that they would have to prove their identities. The will was read. A clerk sat up and called out, "Is there one named Cassia present?" The audience looked around as a hushed mumbling began to rumble toward the front of the makeshift courtroom. "Cassia, would you please come forward, if you are in this room." Cassia walked to the front. She was astonishingly vibrant in her white gown laced with gold and silver. "Are you Cassia?" "Yes, Lord, I am." The clerk asked, "Can you prove your identity?" "I wear the signet ring of Augustus who gave it to me only days before he died. I also have a scroll written by my mother and signed by a priest long ago. See here is my name, Cassia, daughter of Phanuel and Selkah."

The clerk held up the ring and then passed it to every member of the Senate. All agreed that it belonged to the Emperor. "Cassia, to you this day Rome bequeaths two million drachma. You may claim your inheritance at the Treasury of the Vestals." "Now, is there one named Judas here?" Judas answered, "Yes, I am he!" "How shall you prove your identity young man?" Cassia stepped forward and told her the story about Augustus giving her the child and raising it. "Is this all the proof you have?" Cassia answered, "Yes, isn't my testimony enough?" The clerk responded, "No it is not enough. How do we know that this child is indeed Judas the one named in the will? He could be someone else for all we know. You have to find additional evidence to prove his identity. Judas burst into a fit of anger. It was not fair. He should have part of the inheritance too. Red-faced, he sat down and glared at Magdala.

"Magdala, are you sitting in this room?" asked the clerk. "If so, come to the front of the room. Magdala walked forward, "I am she." "Can you prove your identity? Magdala told the story about her parents and how she had been forced to take the oath of the Vestals by Augustus. Then she told them how she escaped from the temple the day the Vestals were burned but did not give the details. She took off her veil to reveal the mark of the Vestal.

Magdala's story sufficiently convinced most of the Senate to vote for her after she had been questioned about the incidence and remembered the names and events very clearly. They voted for her inheritance and rescinded her vows of celibacy. Still there were some who claimed that she was a fraud because Magdala had been burned with the others.

Ecstatically happy Cassia and Magdala came to the Senate with little and left with a fortune. That fortune would take care of them for the rest of their lives if they managed it well. Judas was despondent. "Judas," said Magdala, "don't worry I will give you half of everything I have received. And I am sure Cassia will share with you also." Judas answered sorrowfully, "Thank you for your generosity. I will not take part of your fortune; it is not fair to you. Someday I will find a way to prove my identity and then I will inherit my own fortune."

Meanwhile Judas did have the jewels. No one knew how much they were worth. None of them thought it was the right thing to take the jewels and none of them would divulge that they had stolen the will either. To this very day no one in Rome knew about the riches that were stolen by Judas. Not a single person had even taken inventory of the Treasury and no one, not one person in Rome ever knew that Judas became a very rich man at the expense of the State. In a way, he did receive his inheritance.

It was not too long before Magdala and Dorcas persuaded Judas to leave Rome and return with them to Judea. Cassia retired to her mountain retreat and assured the threesome that her Senator friend would keep her company over the long winter months. She was wealthy now, but for whatever reason, she continued to choose a life of solitude and mysterious liaisons.

CHAPTER TEN
FOLLOWING A STAR

"The Star God will bring happiness to all."

In fire-darkened caves in the scorched desert south of Jerusalem there arose a ray of hope as women and men huddled together staring into the distant night skies. As they grieved for themselves and their imprisoned families, they began to tell stories about a child conceived by a Star. Someday this child would overthrow their oppressors and create a world of peace and prosperity for everyone. They longed for its coming.

This supernatural being came to be known by many names such as the Chose One, the Son of a Star, and the Star God. Thousands believed that they were chosen, that they were following in the path of the Star. Sword in hand they led ruthless and bloody revolts against the mighty Roman army. None of those revolutionaries survived. Some thought they could buy or bargain their way into the power of the Star Child, but they also received the same fate. All who attempted to take power for themselves from Rome were executed.

Magdala gazed out the porthole toward Galilee and wished that she could talk with Lysander. She longed to touch him, to be with him, if only for a moment. It seemed as if she was always wishing for something that she left behind. She left part of herself with Lysander, the wonder worker, the magician.

While on the long and often treacherous journey from Rome to Syrian Antioch, Magdala hid her inheritance in a variety of places on the ship. She had to protect herself from both people on the ship and the captain. Many wealthy people had been lost at sea these days. For the most part, Dorcas, Magdala, and Judas did not leave each other's company. Judas continued to brood while Dorcas made plans to find her brother or his remains. He was the only family that she had left in the world.

Early one morning Magdala began making plans with Judas. "Judas, I have decided to go to Galilee before returning to my position at the Migration office in Caesarea. You go on to Caesarea and I will be there within a month. I can't help it. I have to go back to Galilee. It is as if something keeps calling me. I feel as if part of me is still there. Judas protested, "Magdala, we could go later." "No, I have to go because I want to find a friend." Judas conceded, "If you won't go to Caesarea now, then I will not go either. Who do I know there anyway?" Magdala turned to Dorcas and asked, "Will you go with me too?" Dorcas answered sadly, "No, my dearest, I cannot follow your dreams. I have some of my own. I have to find my brother wherever he is. The best way to do that is to work for the Romans. They have special ways of helping you when you serve them."

Finally they arrived at the port near Antioch in Syria. As they left the ship Dorcas hugged a sobbing Magdala. They had become like sisters and would probably never see each other again. Once more, Magdala made a choice that would take her away from someone she loved dearly. After giving Dorcas her share of Magdala's fortune, Magdala said, "Dorcas, I will travel to Jerusalem as soon as I find my friend. Write and tell me where you are living," asked Magdala. "Magdala," cried Dorcas sheepishly, "How could you not know? I cannot write. My schooling ended when my mother was killed. I know many spoken languages but cannot read any of them. But I will find a way. You will know where I am. Farewell."

On the way from the ship to their Inn near Antioch, Magdala rode with the ship's captain. Explaining her intended itinerary, the captain did not hesitate to conjure up stories of thieves and insane people who attack and maim travelers at night on the road to Capernaum. If Magdala were a prudent woman who valued her life she would obtain the services of a guide. He recommended a few and Magdala found one who was willing to make the unpredictable long journey to the Sea of Galilee.

The next morning, Magdala, Judas and their guide headed south. "It's only a four day's journey, Miss," shouted a husky vice that came from the other side of the camel. "We'll travel by day and set our tents early. You'll like the countryside." Amphion, the guide, seemed capable. He was an average looking man who handled the animals well but did not smell like one of the Herders. "Why do you work as a guide out her in the wilderness?" asked Magdala. "It's a living Miss, and I know these hills as well as my own body. I have traveled through the back roads most of my life." Magdala observed, "Your hands don't look like those of a laborer.

Have you always done this type of work?" "No, Miss," answered Amphion, "long ago I used to sell the stars and play a game for rain." "What do you mean Amphion," asked Magdala. "Miss, I was a gambler of sorts. But after a while it did not pay. So the captain of the vessel you came on helped me to find this type of work."

Magdala worried about this curious man, with such gentle manners and strong speech. And Magdala should have wondered. Amphion used to terrorize travelers in the mountains. Twice he had been caught and punished. Now he safely guides people through the mountains on roads where the thieves would have trouble hiding. Unknown to Amphion some of his old friends were waiting for him a few miles outside of Antioch. They had a score to settle. Amphion had not divided up some of the stash that they had taken years ago. They thought that he had hidden it somewhere. The truth was that the Romans had confiscated it as evidence.

As they rode Magdala thought of Lysander and, oddly, even of John. He had been a good friend and she longed to share with him all her adventures. Lysander seemed to flood her mind. Perhaps she was ready to risk caring for someone again. If she ever found Lysander she was going to tell him that she cared very much for him. Now that she was wealthy she might be able to help him in his work.

The threesome had only been on the road for about six hours when it happened. As quick as lightning something came out of the bushes and knocked them to the ground. Judas clutched at his pack. It contained all of the jewels he had stolen from the Treasury in Rome. In a flash something hit him and he fell to the ground face down. Magdala was pulled from the camel. Someone threw a blanket over her head and twisted leather straps around her hands and feet. She was dazed but she could hear the men and a woman talking. "Amphion, so you thought you could take our money with you? Who do you think you are? Do you think that we would forget you? We would never forget you!"

"Tell us where the goods are and we will spare your life and the two over there." Amphion complained, "I have no money, no goods. The centurions took it as evidence. Didn't you hear? I spent over two years at hard labor in the copper mines for that money. I don't have it." One of the robbers said, "Tell us where you have put it or you die." "I tell you I don't know anything and I don't have any of the goods." "Ahh," screamed Amphion, as a razor sharp blade slid into his stomach. Just as quickly they slit open all of the packs and bags that Magdala and Judas were carrying. "Come here, come over here, look what I found," said one of the robbers.

The robber had torn open Judas' bag. Like crazed animals they threw the jewels and coins in the air. They were rich. What luck! Good ole Amphion did pay them back with plenty. "Shall we kill these two also?" said one of the robbers. "Leave them alone, they will probably die out here in the mountains or maybe someone else will do it for us. They don't know who we are so let's get out of here."

"Oh, ah, ah," moaned Judas. As Judas looked around at the mess, he began to cry. "They have taken it all. They have taken all of it. Nothing is left. Nothing." Magdala cried, "Judas, come over here and help me. Help me out of this thing. I can't move." Judas ran over to help her. "Look, at Amphion, his stomach and mouth ..." as he began to throw up. Judas had been protected all of his life and this was just too much for him. He collapsed in a heap on the ground moaning after untying Magdala. Just as quickly he passed out.

Finally waking up Judas, Magdala told him what happened and how the looters had taken his jewels. "In a way, the jewels and coins saved our lives. They may have killed us." Judas said remorsefully, "Magdala, I have nothing now. I don't even have any clothing to wear. They tore them all to shreds." Magdala lifted up her skirt and there taped to her leg was her own bag of money. "Look, my money is safe. I will divide it with you. I told you all along that whatever I inherit would be yours also."

After burying Amphion, they gathered up their belongings and headed southward along the desolate road to Galilee, stopping only for food and water during the four-day's journey on the camels. They wondered that the robbers did not steal the camels also? Soon they reached the edge of Capernaum, a city in Galilee, just about mid-day. All along their journey, Magdala asked everyone they met, "Do you know of one called Lysander?" All of them knew of a wonder man, a magic man, some called him the Messiah. Some thought that they had heard that name before but they were not positive. Each described a man who did wonderful things for the needy. His activities were well known throughout Judea. She heard stories about him challenging the priests in the temple near his home.

As they approached Capernaum, they could hear what seemed to be thousands of voices. Where were they coming from? Were they out in the desert for too long? As they climbed the huge hill overlooking the sea, they stumbled into what seemed to be a festival. Thousands of happy, singing people met them. They were all eating and dancing. What were they singing? It sounded like, "Lysander is our God, Our new King, Tomorrow we will live again..." Magdala thought, "It can't be. Are they singing about Lysander?" As they pushed through the crowds, Magdala shouted to some of the people, "Where is this Lysander?" All of those who heard pointed to the top of a small hill.

Standing with several men and a few women was Lysander. His blonde hair and slight stature seemed so different from all of the dark-skinned muscular people around him. He looked tired and much older than Magdala remembered. Magdala jumped down off the camel, leaving Judas all alone, and ran toward the top of a small hill. "Lysander, Lysander, it's me Magdala." There were so many people and it was so noisy that he did not hear her. She ran faster and came up to within a few feel of him. As she reached out her arms, she cried, "Lysander, Lysander, it's me Magdala!" Someone yelled, "Get away woman. Don't you see that he is tired? You are only one of thousands. What makes you think he will help you first?"

Several of Lysander's followers pushed her down the hill. Magdala would not give up. With tears in her eyes, she ran up the hill once again. The followers remarked, "Persistent little bitch, isn't she? Lets carry her down the hill!" Just as the men began to lift her into the air, a tall man walked toward them. He did not like what was going on. Standing at least a head taller than all the rest of them, he said, "Put the woman down, now!" The followers responded, "Okay, okay we were just trying to protect Lysander. You know that the women won't leave him alone for a minute." Magdala recognized the man. "John, hello there, it's me, Magdala!" John took a second look. It was Magdala. She was dressed in the finest clothing with beautiful jewels around her head. He had never seen such a beautiful woman.

"Magdala, where have you been? How did you get here?" asked John. "I have come to find Lysander. And they won't let me talk with him," explained Magdala. "Come with me, I will take you to him," encouraged John. John took Magdala by the hand, still sobbing, when they finally stood behind Lysander. "Lysander, Lysander, it is me, your Magdala." Lysander swung around and caught her by surprise. Clutching her in his arms he held on to her like he was never going to let her go. "Magdala, Magdala, I have missed you. I thought that you might have died. Where did you go?" asked Lysander.

Several of the women and men who stood a few yards away began to heckle Magdala. "Who is this woman who claims his attention? What right does she have to him?" In the middle of all of these people Lysander and Magdala held each other. They were in a world all of their own. Lysander felt strengthened inside as he held her. She brought life and energy to his weary soul. "Where are you going Lysander," yelled one of his followers.

He replied with a riddle, "Foxes have holes and birds have nests but I have no where that I can call home. I am going home."

Home for Lysander was Magdala. He had met many women since arriving in Judea. Some offered to live with him, to care for him, to sleep with him, to help him in every way possible. But, he could not forget Magdala. He could not forget the day she summoned power to heal herself. She had the ability to direct his healing power to unite with hers. He knew that she had divinity within her.

Magdala and Lysander were two people who needed each other. Both were searching for something to fill an emptiness inside them. When they met again on the hill in front of more than five thousand witnesses, for a brief moment the emptiness left them. They walked toward the mountains and as they walked they talked and talked. Their insides poured out as they linked their lives and futures together. Magdala remembered Bara again, told of Judas and her recent good fortune. Lysander was physically and mentally exhausted. He had spent all of the past months helping people. He had healed many but could not do anything about how they lived. Many lived on food thrown away by others. Some wrapped themselves in discarded clothes and lived and slept next to the streets. He could heal the body but he could not feed and clothe all of the lost children. An immense pain saturated his body every moment he was awake. His magic was not powerful enough to change the lives of the poor and hungry. Most days, he felt as if he was a failure.

Lysander experienced a never-ending ache inside his soul. The Gods did not seem to care as he did for the people. Admiringly, Magdala listened and studied him. He had aged. His face drew lines of sadness. She reached out her hands and risked, "Come, come to me." And Magdala and Lysander found each other once again. Each touch brought greater moments of ecstasy. As they shared their bodies and souls, each became stronger. They were family for each other. They had found a quiet still assurance of care and commitment. They cried for days. It was as if no one else in the world existed. There were great moments of silence as they both looked into the fire. It was as if time itself had stopped. This was a gift of the Gods.

A morning sun found Magdala and Lysander swimming in the Jordan. Here near the Sea of Galilee the water was cold, clean, and clear, unlike the murky mixture that flowed near Jerusalem after it flowed through miles and miles of desert and people. The upper Jordan refreshed its visitors. Breathing seemed so special to both of them. It was as if they had been reborn, renewed. Together they began to make plans. Magdala had a fortune. She would finance Lysander and his work. If all of Judea wished it, if all the people went to King Herod and threatened to revolt then Lysander could become King. He would change the squalid lives of many of his followers. Instead of building huge palaces, he would give money to the poor.

First Lysander must win the confidence of the people in the north, near Galilee, and then move south towards Jerusalem. He would open his life to all sorts of people. He would cross race, religion, and economic lines. In order for the plan to be successful, Lysander would have to be proclaimed king by popular acclamation. Rome would have to listen to its people then. Rome did not have the resources to take on all of the people of Judea, especially with border wars that were draining the Empire's finances.

Determined, Magdala and Lysander began to plan. Magdala bought a farm outside of Nazareth that served as a retreat for Lysander. Judas, whom Magdala had completely ignored for days, did not share their idealistic dreams of making a better Judea. He agreed to stay on at the house as manager while Lysander and Magdala traveled throughout Judea. For months Magdala and Lysander traveled Galilee. They stopped for everyone they met. Lysander healed everyone that was possible to heal. They saw such poverty; even the Herders lived better than many of the people who begged for their daily crumbs. No one cared for these people. When Lysander showed care and attention to them, the village would anoint him as King. Some claimed that he was indeed the child born of a Star.

His popularity began to escalate. Followers increased daily. Some thought that Lysander would take care of them forever. Others joined his traveling company because they believed he could change the world. They understood the devastating effect that poverty has on people. Others saw Lysander as a tool for their amusement. He would bring them personal wealth and power over others. Lysander's magnetic personality and magical power touched everyone he met. Women found him to be so attractive that they left their homes and families to travel with him. It mattered little that he had no means of supporting himself or that he had no real possessions of his own. They pledged to follow him to the ends of the Empire.

Neither Magdala nor Lysander anticipated the problems that followed such popularity. The crowds near Capernaum seemed small these days. Masses of people moved with him daily. Many others viewed Lysander as a threat. Gradually this group began to grow as they talked about their mistrust and hatred of Lysander with townspeople. He was feeding them a line. He could not do what he promised. One day while healing a blind man in Jerusalem, several hostile people attacked Lysander from behind. Three men with knives were bound and determined to kill him. As they tried to grab Lysander, he shouted, "By the Gods who ordained me to the priesthood, I shall take your souls from you if you do not stop."

His assailants struggled with him even stronger. With a raised hand and open eyes, Lysander demonstrated the secrets of immortality by bringing death to the three. "By the Gods who ordained me, I have warned you. From this moment on your souls will be given to the Nethers. Be gone!" Just as suddenly the three men fell backwards with their eyes toward the clouds. One of the people watching the skirmish stepped forward and touched the bodies. "They are dead. Oh God, they are dead!"

The masses of people heaved a great sigh and stepped backward. One by one the witnesses left until only Magdala and Lysander and the three dead men were left in the street. Magdala, eyes wide open, sighed also. "Lysander, I did not know that you had the power of death." Lysander explained, " Unfortunately one of the lessons of learning the secrets of immortal life is to conquer death. These men are not dead. They have been sent to the Nethers. Someday they will return, perhaps in another body. But they will return. None of those who witnessed this today will understand what has happened here today. Do you believe me Magdala?" Magdala was stunned! The man whom she had watched raise several people from the grips of death had now pronounced that sentence on others. It was too much for her to understand. She thought she knew him. She saw his kind and gentle side but not this. She needed to be alone. She, also, left Lysander standing in the middle of the street.

Lysander, in spite of this incident, became even more popular. The Romans began to watch every move he made and the religious authorities gritted their teeth each time Lysander proved to be more magical and more powerful than they were. The people loved Lysander because he ate and drank with them. Lysander was not afraid of entering their rat-infested makeshift homes and sleeping on their cots. He was a people's King and everyone knew that it was going to happen. Magdala and Lysander's strategies were working. Some of the most powerful people in the cities they visited were afraid to question him, to criticize his magic. They feared that the people would revolt. Rome had stationed thousands of men in Judea. But those soldiers were only a handful when compared to the millions of people who regularly traversed the continent in order to keep religious festivals and pay homage to their Gods in Jerusalem. Lysander would soon be crowned King, it was only a matter of time.

Whether or not Lysander had thought about his mother, no one will ever know. One fine spring day, a day that had been set aside for a marriage between two followers, Mariam appeared. Lysander was drinking a glass of wine with a few of his friends in Cana while Magdala was helping the bride to prepare for the ceremony. Tauntingly, Lysander heard a voice say, "What do you mean, there is no wine?" He turned around and standing next to some of the workers was a finely dressed older woman. She was thin and greying but had a tremendous presence about her. "Why I thought the great magician was at this wedding? Ask him, if he can raise the dead surely he can fill my empty glass of wine?" Lysander responded, "Woman are you referring to me?" She answered, "Are you the great healer that I have been hearing about? Lysander answered, "I don't know. Can you tell me anything about this person?" Mariam obliged, "He used to like to play in the sand outside the great house near Bethlehem, until the Romans took him away from me and sold him to people in the north."

Lysander began to weep. "Mother, is it really you?" With tears rolling down their faces, both embraced and kissed. "It is me. But is it you Lysander? You have changed. You are so different than what I imagined. It is you I know but your eyes are not the eyes of the little boy that was taken from me so long ago. And why is your hair so light?" Lysander explained, "Both my hair and my right eye are signs of the Asclepioi. I was sent to Epidaurus to become a priest."

Mariam began to tell her story, "It seems to long ago and yet only yesterday when they tore my heart out of me. I have looked for you since the day they took you. Every time I saw a child in the street, I wondered if it was you. For years I worked for Roman officials as a slave. They sold me into slavery for another twenty years. I persuaded many of them to help me look for you but none of their efforts worked. Over the years I saved any extra money I was given and was finally able to buy myself out of slavery. A generous Roman statesman arranged to purchase a small cottage for me in Galilee. He said it was because of my service to the state. Only months ago while I was preparing to move to my new home, I heard someone talking about a magician by the name of Lysander. I could not believe my ears. I asked her about the magician but she only knew about the things he had done. She knew nothing about his background. So I heard that you were going to be in Cana today, and I came here to see if you were indeed my Lysander."

"Mother, I can't believe this is happening. You will have to come home with us tonight. Please come meet Magdala, the other person in my family." Magdala was also surprised. Lysander had never spoken of Mariam. She assumed that his mother was dead or that he had been an orphan. All of them shared an evening meal and talked about their hopes and dreams for Lysander. Mariam remembered how she had dreamed of her child being a great person some day. Yet, she feared for Lysander. "Aren't you afraid that the Romans will arrest you? They could condemn you to death in an instant," asked Mariam. "Mother, they have to present evidence. I heal many people and no one could prove that I have done or said anything about being a King. I have been very careful." Mariam warned, "You should have people around you who can protect you." Lysander tried to explain to her, "Mother, you do not understand. I am a priest of Asclepius, I do not need to be protected."

Mariam agreed to travel with the group for a few days. Lysander was heading toward Jerusalem in the morning. To be with her son, she agreed to go, even though she feared for his life and even hers. After her trek with Lysander to Jerusalem, she returned home to Nazareth. What began in the minds of Lysander and Magdala as an idealistic quest on behalf of people who needed help transformed into something very different. Followers wanted power. They would hang around in the evenings and quarrel over who would have this position or that position when Lysander became King. And Lysander was changing also. He was not healing as many people and it seemed as if he was making more speeches. And the more he talked, the more he sounded like someone who wanted to be more than a healer. He would say, "Put away the old, try the new," and "Don't sew new patches on old garments."

There was a sense of expectation in the air. Everyone could feel it. Something was about to happen. The people feverishly waited for Lysander everywhere he went. And as they waited, they pushed and shoved one another. When traveling, Lysander never had a quiet moment. Everyone knew who he was and they were all coming to the same conclusion. Lysander will be a King and give freedom to the people at last. He will make a new kingdom that will take away our pain and suffering.

Lysander felt the same fever. He had the same disease. He began waking up in the middle of the night. Often he would go for days without sleep and when he did finally sleep he would awake drenched with sweat. The recurring nightmare was when he looked into the mirror and saw only blackness, darkness. This darkness frightened him. Magdala tried to calm him. But her words and body seemed to have less and less of a healing effect on him. He was changing and Magdala did not understand the reasons for those changes.

During the day he welcomed the company of female followers. Often he would take them up into the mountains alone. He liked their attention and enjoyed the freedom away from the dirt and stench of the streets. His male followers began to feel alienated and alone. Lysander had very little time for them any longer. Years of healing street people had taken its toll on Lysander. He needed to get away or to find a quiet place for himself. The great void that Magdala had filled was fading. Lysander began to search again. He wanted to be King more than anything else in life. He began to believe that it was his destiny. On one of his journeys into Jerusalem people shouted, "Welcome King Lysander, Hosanna! Welcome to the son born of a Star." Villagers began talking about Lysander constantly. They charted his every move. He had become their Star child. He was the ancient one predicted by all the sages and he was now in their lives.

In spite of Lysander's gradual withdrawal from her, Magdala continued to take care of his financial obligations. And Lysander seemed to need her money less and less. After all there were other women who wanted to share their personal belongings with him too. Lysander attracted the very rich who appeared to have a social conscience. They contributed generously to his work. For their gifts they demanded part of him, time with him. And he was willing to give to them. It was so much easier than facing the starving, sick people in the alleys and infested cottages. Yet Lysander always came back to Magdala. Every evening, no matter what he had done or where he had been, he would come back to her. They belonged to each other.

One hot night Magdala fell asleep before Lysander returned. She dreamed about a dark road leading nowhere. As she walked she called out for Lysander. She could not find him. Along the road she noticed a trail of blood. She began to follow it. Suddenly as she looked up she saw only a hand of Lysander. It was limp. She began to weep and as she wept she stretched out her hand toward his. All of a sudden the hand turned to a bright star that exploded and trailed across the sky falling to the earth. Magdala woke up panting, "Lysander, Lysander."

CHAPTER ELEVEN
THE LETHAL WISH

"Love's wishes sometimes kill us."

Like a flash of light on the horizon before a storm, Vanya son of Sacharia came blazing across the Jordan River. Vanya, so they say, was celibate. He had been brought up among the Zadokites in their retreat at Qumran but had rejected their ways, choosing a wandering life in the desert. No sane woman would ever want to share her life with the likes of this man. He was brazen, unshaven, and hair hanging down to his shoulders. By the time he was thirty, his beard nearly touched the ground. Wearing only hides of animals, his hairy arms and hands supported ten- inch fingernails. Like a bad omen, his voice thundered over the mountains into the valleys below.

Vanya came out of the dust of nowhere and claimed that he had secret knowledge of the Child born of a Star. Zealously he predicted the Child's arrival. Verbally assaulting and accosting every passerby, he would shout, "The Star is coming. Prepare yourselves. The time has come. Change your lives now while you still have time." Vanya lived by the rigid standards set down by one called Mashua. Mashua was an ancient leader who demanded a strict ascetic lifestyle. Followers ate only desert creatures and fruit, lived in caves, and never married or mated. For Mashua this was the best life a person could have. It was pure and without the touch of a tainted and spoiled civilization.

Vanya would stand out in the middle of the marketplace and preach chastity and celibacy. He abhorred those who wasted money at the expense of someone else who had nothing. Some said that he was the coming Star but others thought he was a hoax. Still it was hard not to listen to him when he spoke. Like Lysander his words and ways threatened many. The rich were his prime target for they were the ones who corrupted the rest of the world.

On a dusty day one summer evening Magdala escaped to the Jordan river where she could bathe alone. Stepping into the water, Magdala could hear an animal breathing in the brush. Suddenly something bounded toward the water. She screamed but no one could hear her. "Who is here? Come out and show yourself." She heard nothing only erratic breathing. Quickly she climbed to the shore and pulled a shawl over her wet body. "Who is there? I demand that you come out of there at once!" To Magdala's surprise coming toward her very slowly was an animal that looked like a man. She screamed with all her might, "Ahhh, someone help me! Help Me!"

Magdala was too far from the camp for anyone to hear her. So she gritted her teeth, picked up a piece of wood, and waited for the attack. She was going to face this monster even if she was alone. "Magdala, don't you remember me? the monster said quietly? "What, no I don't. I've never met you before and I know I would have remembered you." Just as sweetly and quietly the very large man came over and sat down in front of Magdala. "Magdala, I remember you. Years ago you visited the commune of the Zadokites." She answered, "Yes, many people knew that I went there." "I was one of the brothers who lived high above in the caves. You even came into my cave. Elder brought you there. Do you remember?" Magdala came back at him, "Yes, not too long after that I was captured by Herders and barely escaped with my life." The man continued, "Do you remember finding a scroll by your bedroll on the morning that you left?" Magdala answered, "Yes, I thought that was very odd—someone came into my tent while I was sleeping." The man explained, "Actually, you were drugged. Elder was afraid that you were going to tell the Romans about their plans. You seemed too interested in what was going on in the settlement. I convinced him not to harm you while you were at the commune. But he would not listen to me and so sent for the Herders. He set the trap for you."

"I left the scroll in your tent so that you would see that most of us were harmless. We all wanted a new King but there were many of us who did not believe in a violent revolution. We were awaiting the arrival of someone who would lead us to victory peaceably. The very night you arrived at Qumran, the brothers were planning to attack Roman soldiers stationed at a place called Masada in the desert."

Magdala snarled, "It is very difficult for me to believe that all of that was happening right before my eyes and I did not see it. The man replied, "You did not want to see it." Magdala angrily faced the man, "Why didn't you help me when we were kidnapped by the Herders?" "I could do nothing. I was only a novice then and I had sworn to obey the Elder. I would have been thrown out of the community if I did not listen to him. I had no place to go. Shortly after my mother and sister were carried off by the Herders, my father died on the streets of Bethlehem. He had spent all of his money searching for them. Life was pointless to him without my mother and sister. At his burial, outside the city, a kindly old man approached me. In exchange for work, he offered me food and a place to live. Many of the inhabitants of Qumran were orphans who came to live with them because so few men chose to live a celibate life in the desert. We live with them and they teach us their ways of life. In return we help them in whatever way we can. At the age of thirty they allowed me to choose to stay with them or leave. I left."

Magdala quizzed him. "Your sister was kidnapped and your mother too?" He replied, "Yes, a very long time ago." "By Herders?" "Yes, I told you...," Magdala continued, "Are you the first born of Sacharia?" He answered, "How did you know that?" Magdala ran toward the man and hugged him. "You are the brother of Tabitha." "Who?" he said. "She calls herself Dorcas now. I can hardly believe that I am talking with you. Your sister is alive and well. Well, the last time I saw her she was. She has returned to Jerusalem to find you and is probably searching for you at this very moment. We had heard that the Romans had killed you." "What do you call yourself?" "Magdala!" "They call me "Vanya."

Magdala ran over behind some of the brush and put on her clothing. Together they sat together on the shore talking about their lives and especially Dorcas. Because of their experiences, Magdala and Dorcas had grown very close, as close as sisters. She told him about how ferocious Dorcas had been in the desert and helped her in many adventures. As the day wore on, it became so dark that they could hardly see each other. Magdala held out her hands to Vanya, "Come back to the tent with me. We have food and you must meet Lysander."

So the gentle monster followed Magdala to the tents. They were greeted with such "oohs and aahs" that Magdala laughed out loud. You would have thought that she had captured a wild animal. Several followers spit on them and told them to leave. Ignoring their insults, Magdala made her way toward Lysander who was talking with a few followers near the edge of a clearing. Magdala approached him, "Excuse me Lysander, I want you to meet Vanya." Lysander stared at him. He could not move. Something stirred inside him as if he had met this thing before at another time in another world. He was almost paralyzed and could barely say, "Who are you?"

Vanya answered, "I am Vanya from across the river," as his voice reached the clouds. Lysander said, "I have heard of you. Some of your followers say that you want to be King. Many of them have joined with us. They say that they are afraid of you." Vanya answered back, "I only want to change the ways of those who ignore all of the dying and starving people in the streets. If my followers leave me that is their choice. They will have to suffer with that decision. I have heard about you also Lysander."

For most of the evening they talked about their hopes and dreams for Judea. Lysander and Vanya kept feeling the strange kinship, like distant souls caught in the same time and space. Vanya believed that Lysander was the Child born of the Star. The next morning Vanya said farewell and headed off to Jerusalem. Within four days, he was imprisoned by Herod. Vanya had criticized Herod's unusual love life and for that public statement, Herod sentenced him to the dungeons. He wanted to kill him but he was afraid that his followers would storm the palace.

It was in one of the dismal cells that Dorcas found Vanya on the day before he was murdered. Dorcas had overheard a maid at the palace telling Vanya's story. It had to be her brother. After finding him and taking care of his wounds she went back to her residence to sleep for a while. When she returned the next day she found his body heaped in a garbage pile outside the palace. As a practical joke, one of Herod's lovers had Vanya's head brought to him stuffed in the belly of a bird.

Enraged Dorcas vowed to kill the royal family. Pretending to be a server, she managed to sneak into the royal dining area the next day. Knife in hand she lunged toward the King only to be stopped by the Royal Guards who later took her to Caesarea and used her for sport in the theatre. News of Vanya's murder spread throughout the countryside. Herod denied that he had anything to do with it. He claimed that others had beaten Vanya to death in the dungeon. Magdala feared for their lives as followers flocked to Lysander. Everyone was uneasy and afraid that war was coming.

Back in Galilee Judas kept busy managing Magdala's farm near Nazareth. It was meant to be a retreat for Lysander and Magdala but in the past three years they had visited it infrequently. Consequently the house became a haven and sanctuary for those who followed Lysander. Many of them could not travel the distance to the desert and beyond. They stayed in Galilee and took care of those who needed longer to recover from their illnesses. Not all who received the touch of Lysander were cured instantly.

Over the years the small villa became noted for healers and practitioners of the ways of Lysander. No longer did they want to call themselves followers of the ancient ways of an Asclepioi priest. Some of them did not even know that much of their training given by Lysander in his earlier years was the same that he had received at Epidaurus. Houses like Magdala's began to sprout up all over Galilee. Many of the affluent women and men who had been healed by or befriended by Lysander opened their homes to the weary or homeless. Lysander's magic was reaching more and more people. It was only a matter of time before he would be acclaimed King.

One evening Magdala approached Lysander, "I am going home to Nazareth. I need to rest. Judas will come and take my place while I am gone." Lysander was frantic. "Magdala, how can you leave me now. The moment is coming. It will be any day. Don't you want to see the celebration when they anoint me King?" Magdala tried to explain, "Lysander, I have grown weary of all of the people. I am afraid, there has been talk of war. The Romans have been training troops in the Megiddo Valley. And look what happened to Vanya and Dorcas. They have only been gone a few weeks. You could be next." Lysander pleaded with her, "Have faith in me. I know what I am doing. You have seen only some of my powers. Do you think that they could stand against me? Besides, I have done nothing illegal. I merely heal those who ask. Rome will not provoke the people. It would mean an all-out revolution."

Magdala strongly said again, "I am leaving. I will be away for a few months. Judas will find you in a few days. He will take care of you. Goodbye my love." Magdala put her arms around Lysander and held on. She did not want to leave him for she had invested almost all of her fortune and her life over the past few years. Leaving him was like tearing herself into bits. It seemed as if her whole being ached as she turned to leave. Lysander meant everything to her. But lately she had been having the fevers again. His touch could not help her any longer. He was not the same magician she met so many years ago. His gentle touch brought only grief not health these days. She knew that her grieving had only begun. Lysander had left her, and in a way, and when and if he was crowned King, she would never be a part of his life again. Lysander called to her, "Hurry back soon! You will see that life will be better for all of us soon."

Magdala knew the Romans better than Lysander. They had schooled her. Becoming King was not just a matter of public acclaim; the Romans never give up anything without a fight. Judas agreed to join Lysander after Magdala returned to Nazareth. He was now excited to be a part of Lysander's group. The idea of being with royalty appealed to him. Yet, he never camped with Lysander when they entered a town or a burrow. While Lysander visited the sick, Judas went off to explore the town or countryside on his own. In his secluded existence, he never really experienced how people lived. He knew that there was poverty but he had never seen such filthy living conditions. Visiting the poor towns made him feel superior. He was better educated, had more money, and even if it was Magdala's money, was a gentleman, and a citizen of the state.

Everywhere Lysander traveled, Judas enjoyed the finer things of the villages. Frequenting the local Inns usually occurred after a long day of haggling in the marketplace. And Judas loved he women, but they apparently did not love him. Even when he bought them very expensive presents, they never swarmed around him like they did around Lysander. Lysander did not have to look for the women, they found him. And they brought gifts to him. Judas winced every time he saw the herd of women that followed Lysander. What did he have? What made him so irresistible? Judas had no designs on being King himself. Why that was too much responsibility. Be he did like the idea of the wealth it might bring him. If Lysander was crowned King, Judas thought that his life would improve. Women would want him then.

The day finally came when several hundred followers planned to anoint Lysander as their King. They knew that Rome would retaliate but they were willing to risk it. The followers had one thing going for them, if Lysander was not allowed to rule as King, all of Jerusalem would revolt. By nightfall the graveyard across from the city glowed with anxious and hungry revolutionaries. The time had arrived!

Now Judas loved Lysander in his own way. Occasionally Judas' anger would flare over Lysander's popularity with the women, but even so, he admired the man. He wanted to make him King just as much as anyone. He had heard that some of the followers were planning to sabotage the plans to anoint him King. Rome had stationed extra soldiers in Jerusalem and if a revolution broke out, many people would surely die. Some followers argued that it was the wrong time. They should waiting until fall during the festivals when there were more people in Jerusalem. Judas did not like this kind of talk and developed a plan of his own.

Judas believed that Lysander would have the power to defend himself against anyone or anything. He had heard stories from Magdala and others who had witnessed firsthand the magic of his unusual feats of healing. Secretly Judas ran to the entrance of the palace. He knocked on the gate. "I have to see the King of Judea, Agrippa," he screamed to the Centurions. "Fella, get away from here, are you mad? It's late! Everyone is sleeping," yelled one of the Centurions. "I must see him. Tell him it is about another King who will be crowned tonight."

The soldier ran into the garrison and within twenty minutes Judas was in the hallway addressing King Agrippa. Judas told him that Lysander was going to be crowned by a throng of followers that very evening just outside of Jerusalem. The King immediately dispatched several hundred military guards. Turning to Judas, the King handed him a bag full of gold. Judas was surprised, "What is this?" The King answered, "Payment for your information." Judas dropped the bag, "I do not want this!" The King picked it up and handed it to him again, "This is yours. Take it and leave the palace through the garrison at once. You will have to identify the man you have described. As soon as you have done this, you should leave the city and hide in the mountains. You will be a very unpopular man by morning."

Judas led the soldiers to the camp where everyone had gathered. Those who were about to anoint Lysander were not surprised to see Roman officers standing around them. Judas walked up to Lysander as he pushed aside a few soldiers and took Lysander by the hand. "Judas, what is happening?" asked Lysander. "Your time has come!" answered Judas. And with a gesture of lifting his arms in front of Lysander the Romans arrested him. Lysander raised his own arms and they stepped back. But then all of a sudden his arms fell. Judas yelled, "What is the matter. Use your powers. Stop them! Stop them!"

Lysander said nothing. Like a humbled man, he was led away by the soldiers. At that very moment the crowed exploded. Judas ran back into town. He looked for a messenger to take a note to Magdala. He wrote, "Magdala, Lysander has been arrested. Come quickly, he needs you. There is something wrong with him. Judas." Paying the messenger with some of the gold from the King, the young man rode all night. When Magdala received the message she called one of her servants to help her pack and headed south. It took her almost an entire day to reach Jerusalem. When she arrived, she had heard that Lysander had been sent to court already and found guilty of treason. He was to die at noon. She ran to a small rise near Jerusalem, thousands of people were milling about the city waiting for something to happen.

Lysander had a rope around his neck and was standing on the top tier of a gallows. She ran toward him screaming, "Lysander, do you hear me?" Amazingly about all the noise in the crowd, she felt as if Lysander were speaking to her. She continued screaming, "Use your powers. Think about your past and the Asclepioi. I have seen this power in you. Use it! " All she could hear, or what she thought she could hear was, "I can't." The executioner released the lever dropping Lysander into a hole with a huge rope tightened. Within seconds he was dead.

Magdala could not believe what was happening. Neither could the throngs of people watching the execution. How could this happen so quickly and with that thought she collapsed to the ground. (No one knew what really happened that day except the Nethers. Long ago Lysander had promised the Nethers ten years of his life as payment for the knowledge of immortality. He did not know that it took ten years to learn the secret. He thought he had already paid the price they demanded but they chose to take the last ten years of his life. At the very moment when he could have saved himself and been crowned King, the Nethers took away his powers and human life.)

Hundreds of frenzied people watched Lysander die. Their King was dead. They had lost their hopes for the tomorrows. The Star Child had been murdered by Rome. They would revenge his death somehow. For days after the death of Lysander the streets were alive with fires and fights broke out between Roman soldiers and the locals. Tensions kept growing. People were afraid to walk the streets even in the daylight. This enmity would soon give birth to a full-scale war.

Judas had rescued Magdala and taken her to a tent site outside the city. There they consoled each other. No one knew what happened but they all blamed Judas. The more they talked about that night when Lysander was arrested the more Magdala and close followers of Judas hated him. They were not the only ones who hated him. One night, about three days after the hanging of Lysander, an unruly mob marched out of Jerusalem carrying torches. Angrily one of them came within the edge of the huge camp and shouted, "Send Judas to us. We want to talk with him!" Judas did not know why they wanted him. As he approached them, he recognized most of them. They were followers of Lysander and many of them were his friends. Judas asked, "What do you want with me? One of the taller followers answered, "Weren't you the one who led the Romans to Lysander the night he was arrested? Deny it, but we know you were the one."

With a mighty rush of hungry human flesh they clubbed Judas to the ground. And then one by one, they took a stone and threw it at him until his body was completely destroyed. Magdala screamed and tried to stop them but there was nothing she could do. They threatened to kill her too. With all her heart she wished that she had not taken him away from his secure home in Rome. The next morning, what was left of Judas' body was thrown down the cliffs west of Jerusalem. It was a sign of the end of

Jerusalem.

CHAPTER TWELVE
A BRIGHT MOON

"The moon can hypnotize us."

Some people search for the sun because of its warmth that heals and sustains. Others like Magdala find solace in the cool beams of the evening sun, the moon. Even on a cloudy night, rays from the moon can light up a path and help a traveler find her way. These days Magdala found the moon more soothing than the glaring light of the hot desert sun. Magdala could feel nothing. Judas her brother and Lysander her lover were dead. They were gone, she felt lost. Facing an empty future, she returned to her cottage in Nazareth.

About a month after the murders of Judas and Lysander, John the son of Zebedee came to visit Magdala. After Judas' murder and threats by the Romans of destroying other cities, followers of Lysander hid for fear of their own lives. Agrippa had issued a decree that all of the Lysander's followers were to be arrested and interrogated. Several had been jailed and beaten, some were tortured. John came to Magdala for comfort. He too felt a great void. His dreams had died with Lysander. John had also loved Lysander as much as anyone could. Magdala invited him into her home and warned, "John, it is too dangerous to travel." And John defended himself, "I needed to talk with you. I miss Lysander, I dream of him talking to me. I learned so much from him. For the past four years I have known nothing but Lysander and his wishes. He has been my life. I gave up everything for him."

Magdala understood, "I, too, have spent the past few years helping Lysander. He was my life also. I spent much of my fortune on him. He gave so much but then he needed so much himself. I gave and gave to him but in the last few months of his life he had very little time for me. He wanted me to travel with him but he was gone most of the time. It seemed as if the notion of becoming King had captured him." John continued, "You know Magdala, when I first met Lysander, I thought his teachings and way of life were the answer to everything. I thought he could help people in the villages to lead better lives. He embodied all that I wanted to be, a perfect human being. Every day I saw him reach out toward the unhappy, devastated or ill. He was like no other healer. I loved him. Yes, Magdala, we were all idealists." "Idealists?" retorted Magdala.

Magdala and John continued talking and when the sun rose the next morning they were still talking. Other people in the house found them in the garden; they did not even know what time it was. They had been reliving their lives with Lysander. Every story they told was as if he had never left. The stories seemed to keep him in their lives. It was as if he had never left them. John stayed another day and announced he would be leaving in the morning. After dinner in the evening, Magdala and John found a quiet place on the grounds where they could talk. Leaning over toward Magdala, John put his arm on her shoulder. At his touch Magdala trembled. Weeping, she wrapped her arms around John. A tear dropped upon Magdala's hair from John's wincing eyes.

They were two needy people who found comfort in each other. Magdala was not afraid. She saw a love and care in John's eyes that she had never seen in another man's eyes, even Lysander's. She touched him. He was beautiful. Underneath his rough woolen coat was a body of a young and vivacious man. No one loved her the way John did that night in the grass by the light of the moon. Making love quenched the emptiness and ache in their lives. Both had lost a friend and a brother but now they had found each other. It was worth preserving. So they shared their bodies over and over again until the dew of the morning found them fast asleep clutching to each other.

Awakened by thunder of a distant storm, Magdala and John walked arm and arm back to the house. Over breakfast they began to talk about others who might be grieving. Magdala and John arranged a meeting of several friends and followers of Lysander in a cave just outside the ruins of Jerusalem. It would be risky but they wanted to see their friends. Within a month over a hundred people knew about the meeting. John heard that his father was ill and needed to go help him. "I will come to the meeting if I can. Magdala, I don't know what else to say to you!" Magdala knew that she loved John. His visit had given her the strength to begin to reach out to others again. Planning a reunion of Lysander's followers helped her to focus on the future and not the loss of Lysander.

Secret meetings began springing up all over Judea. Even Mariam, Lysander's mother came to a few. When her son died so did her future and past also. Every time she saw Lysander she could see her Egyptian lover. The day she discovered Lysander again was the day that her life was rekindled. The old feelings of adventure into the unknown were hers again. She felt as young as she did with her first romance. Now he was gone and she had no hope. She grieved more for the loss of her dream than her son. Some say that she grieved herself to death. One day she just stopped eating and within a month she died in her sleep.

Magdala would not allow despair to destroy her. People began looking forward to listening to Magdala talk about Lysander and his life. Those that met often began to call themselves the "Servants of Lysander," or the "Servants of the Star Child." There were even some reports that the spirit of Lysander had entered followers or visited them. The more that people talked about these visitations the more people wanted to come to the meetings. Within a year after the death of Lysander, there were at least fifty thousand people who claimed to be followers of the Star Child.

In the process of remembering the words and acts of Lysander, followers began to see that they could themselves be a changing force in Judea. They did not need a King or a miracle worker to make life better for them. They could do it on their own. So the wealthy and the poor, those indentured or free, and males and females came together to help each other. It was a special time. Life began to change as followers and their friends began to take in the homeless, the sick, and the deranged once again. Nazareth became the planning hub of activity and these days rarely did a beggar walk the streets.

Agrippa II watched silently as the meetings grew, knowing that his father had killed Lysander. Secrecy was giving way to open meetings in the name of Lysander. Herod Agrippa II decided it was time to punish the traitors and ordered that all of Lysander's followers detained, whipped, and sentenced to death.

In the early planning of the meetings Magdala enjoyed all of the people but as the numbers grew the work also grew and all of it became a drudgery. The meetings were stale. She had said everything that she could say about Lysander but it was not enough for his ardent followers. She was living out of tents again and wanted to return home to Nazareth. It was not that she had forgotten Lysander, it was that she was very tired and the fevers had returned again. Besides all of that, she was pregnant. Magdala knew about her pregnancy for a long time but told no one. She was afraid that it was all a mistake. She had never even considered having a child or being a mother. When she slept with Lysander, she knew that she would never become pregnant because of his vow to Asclepius and the potion he drank. After escaping the Herders, all of the physicians told her that she would never be able to have children. Bara had given her a disease that consumed her womb. If she did become pregnant it would be a great risk in her life.

Yet Magdala was happy about her pregnancy. The child would be a sign of love and hopeful future. She looked forward to it almost as much as she had looked forward to seeing Lysander after her trip to Rome so many years ago. John visited her often and each time he proposed marriage. Gossip was at a fever pitch in Nazareth about Magdala and John. Magdala was not married and pregnant. She was not a young girl that could be forgiven. Most of the gossip came from women who were afraid that Magdala, the rich and beautiful woman that lived in the hills outside of Nazareth, was sleeping with their husbands. Spitefully, they called her Demimonde. Secretly, they wished that they could be as independent and resourceful as Magdala. They remembered Lysander fondly and Magdala marred that memory of him.

Once again John was visiting Magdala and she questioned him, "Why do you want to marry me?" John patiently answered again, "You have heard the people talk in the village. And you know I love you. I worship you." "But John, I cannot move and live with you and your family. I could never live with your mother and father," cried Magdala. Persuasively John negotiated, "I will you build you a separate house. They will not bother you. You will see that your life will be good." Magdala went on, "John, you do not have that kind of money. I am still a wealthy woman, your family would never forgive you." John argued, "I have saved enough money for the bride price, I can afford you." Magdala laughed, "To whom would you pay this money? I am not like the other women in the village. I do not have a father to whom you could give the money. I love you John but I won't be bought. I am not for sale at any price. We can continue as we are. You can come and visit me whenever you are free from your family business."

John complained, "But, Magdala, the child is mine too!" "John, you can help me raise the child. I cannot become your wife or the possession of any man. I have experienced losing everything for the sake of someone I loved. I will never do that again. Neither can I promise to stay in this house near Nazareth. I dream of seeing Rome and Philip's daughters again."

John continued the argument, "I wouldn't mind if you traveled."

Magdala tried to explain, "I may be gone for months, perhaps a year at a time." John said, "I would agree to it, if you will marry me." Magdala cut to the heart of the matter, "I love you but I know it would be too difficult for you to wait for me to return. Think of how your family would treat you and the townspeople would gossip. It might even hurt your father's business." Sorrowfully, John said, "I cannot win. Whatever you wish is acceptable to me. But Magdala, listen to me; I will never let you go. I will wait for you and if you go away I will find you and bring you back to me. I will never let you out of my life, I promise."

So John was there the day the midwife helped Magdala give birth to a little girl. Magdala called her Phoebe. Each time she called out to the little girl she would remember the moonlite night that John and she shared that brought Phoebe into the world. Her name meant "bright moon."

The months swept by like an old woman-cleaning house. Occasionally Magdala would travel to Rome or some other distant place, always leaving Phoebe behind. John relished the time that he had with the little girl. Slowly, Magdala, John, and Phoebe became a family. Unwilling to return to her old job or to work for the Roman government, Magdala had begun an import business that brought in goods to Nazareth from around the Empire. Her ability to speak several languages helped her. Her clients were usually wealthy and she catered to their requests for certain types of goods. Sometimes she would spend months searching in Egypt or Asia for special furniture or clothing. She loved the travel and it helped to bolster her success.

The followers of Lysander seemed so distant to her now. For fear of their lives many of them had fled to Asia and were known to have traveled as far north as Antioch in Pisidia. Judea was not a safe place to live any longer. Magdala was so unaware of this danger the day she traveled to Jerusalem to check on a shipment from Persia. Traders were to have brought the goods across the great desert by camel. She had heard such revolution talk for years but ignored the warnings to stay out of Jerusalem. John was traveling to Ephesus on business for his father, so she decided to leave five-year-old Phoebe with John's mother. After all, she would only be gone for a few days.

Unknown to Magdala, about a year before she traveled to Jerusalem, revolutionaries had attacked Roman recruits in the desert. Vespasian, one of the most powerful generals in the Roman army was attacked while he slept by terrorists from the desert. Thousands of young recruits were killed in this unprovoked raid and several military machines were stolen. Barely escaping with his life, Vespasian vowed to return to Jerusalem and destroy it.

Returning home to Rome, the people greeted him as a God and affirmed the anointing of him as Emperor by his own troops. Within the month, Vespasian dispatched his son Titus to keep his vow. Jerusalem would soon feel the crushing weight of the mighty Roman army. There had been talk of sporadic fighting near Nazareth, but Magdala ignored all of the rumors. No dead bodies had fallen at her doorstep. Over the years she had heard thousands of rumors and Roman soldiers had been stationed throughout Judea for a long, long time. As she traveled south, she thought nothing of the recruits marching in the Megiddo Valley.

Within twenty-four hours after entering the gates to the city of Jerusalem, Titus surrounded the city and cut off its food and water supply. Magdala found herself in the middle of a war with a city under siege.

CHAPTER THIRTEEN
A GOD-FORSAKEN PLACE

"The Gods were on vacation when Titus arrived."

Jerusalem protected its people by surrounding their homes, businesses, and places of worship with a wall as thick as two chariots. Jutting out over several hills, even modern Roman weapons could not scale two-thirds of the fortification. Locals knew that they could withstand any assault as long as they kept the northern wall intact. Clenched fists met Titus the day he surrounded Jerusalem. Determined to keep their city and their freedom, volunteers fought day and night to protect their city.

Titus knew that over 300,000 people sought refuge behind the impenetrable walls. If his army of mercenaries could continue the fighting, he knew he would conquer Jerusalem. From the day he surrounded the city until its last gasp of breath, no food or water passed its gates. Although under siege, the first days of the war found people dancing in the streets. Confident that they would soon find their freedom or overcome the Romans, most paid little attention to the noise. By the end of the week, shopkeepers had closed their doors and the marketplace had disappeared. Fearing a long siege, people began to hoard food and water. By the end of the month, the stench of rotting flesh penetrated every house and every street. Most homes had run out of food two weeks earlier and the pool of Siloam's supply of water was not enough for the great city.

On the eve of the thirtieth day of fighting Magdala was one of the unlucky ones, she was still alive. Since the first sounds of conflict, Magdala had taken refuge underneath a staircase leading up to the palace. Huddled together they shared what little bits of food and water that could be combed in the streets. Luck had sent them two rats, a wounded bird, and several large insects. People were so desperate that they had taken to chewing on their belts and shoes. Even the straw roofs were used to make soup.

Magdala met her companion during the first week of the siege. Scoundrels had begun roaming the city stealing from the old and the sick. No one could stop them. "Hey lady, you sure are pretty. What you got under that skirt?" Magdala's friend screamed, "Leave me alone! I don't have anything that belongs to you. " The scoundrels kept coming after her, "Come on little honey, let me see under them skirts. I bet you have some food all rolled up inside those soft legs of yours." In an instant, the large men had dragged her off into a corner of the street and began ripping off her clothing. Over twenty people heard her cries but did nothing. No one wanted to risk being attacked by the healthy and virile men. It was survival of the fittest. Spectators began to surround the attack. Like zombies they watched the men abuse her.

The woman began to kick and scream for help. One of the burley men took out a knife and held it at her neck. "Woman, you squirm an inch and you won't squirm any longer." Magdala just happened to be walking by when she heard the woman scream. This time she could not walk by without doing anything. She had seen it before. After the assault, witnesses would tear the body to shreds.

This woman was still alive. In a dance fit for the devil, one by one the men began to rape her. Magdala could not let this happen. Standing in front of the blacksmith, she noticed a huge metal container where molten sludge was kept. The blacksmith looked robust compared to the rest of the scavengers in the streets. On one side of his shop were stacks of swords and weapons. Grabbing the hot metal barrel, Magdala's sizzling hands pushed it until it fell to the ground. Suddenly a huge cloud of smoke poured forth as the fiery lava flow headed toward the frenzied witnesses and the attackers. "Ahh, my feet are burning," screamed the a man who was watching the execution. Screams were heard clear across the city as the spectators quickly dispersed letting the flow hit the men who were scrambling in the dirt. "Damn, Damn, I am burnt," screamed one of the rascals as the other let out a war cry that could not be translated.

Swearing and holding out their arms the two men limped off down the street as the hot metal continued to burn most of the front side of their bodies. Magdala ran over to the woman who was trying to pick herself up from the hot liquid. One entire side of her body was in flames. Magdala shook her, "Are you alright? Talk to me? Where do you live? Where can I take you?" Magdala tore off one of her skirts and began wiping the burned skin. By evening she had carried the woman to the pool of Siloam where she had washed her wounds. The unconscious woman lay like this for almost a week with Magdala by her side.

Unfortunately both of the women were dying. It would not be too long before their pain would end. Early one morning the woman who had been raped opened her eyes and called out, "Flavius, Flavius, is that you?" A startled Magdala answered, "Hello, I am Magdala, there is no Flavius here. I am sorry, Flavius is not here but I am. What do you want? The injured woman cried, "Please help me, it hurts so much." Magdala soothed the woman, "Yes, I know that you have been very ill." The woman again, "What happened to me? All I can remember is those horrid men." Magdala tried to explain, "I managed to stop them but in the process you were badly burned on your right leg," as she pointed to the bandages.

Weak but determined to live, both of the women found a place where they were protected from others wandering the streets. Magdala learned that the woman's name was Chora and she was calling for her son. (Unknown to both of them, Flavius was camped with Titus just outside the city walls.) Flavius Josephus was a general in the Judean army who was captured by the Romans. In exchange for his life he agreed to write about the Roman incursions or wars. Most of the people of Judea thought he was a coward but it did not matter to Chora, she knew that her son had done the right thing. He had saved his own life, hadn't he?

The next two weeks drug on as the two pitiful creatures found very little to eat. Rumors were that many were scaling the walls or sneaking out of the city at night. Some of these poor souls were marched back to the city gates by Titus, usually missing a limb or several fingers. A few of the wealthy walking dead in Jerusalem swallowed their precious stones or gold and turned on the people by informing Titus of happenings within the city. They were desperate for a hot meal but they usually died a horrible death. By chance, mercenaries caught a couple of them picking through their own excrement on the edge of the camp. They were finding gold. It did not take very long for the soldiers to storm the camp of these traitors and cut open their stomachs and intestines. The bloody mess made the soldiers wealthy as they collected all the treasures from the dying bodies.

The world had come to an end. Magdala prayed for death. The streets were littered with thousands of people who had died in their footsteps looking for even a blade of grass to eat. In the midst of this calamity a baby was born. Its mother had no milk to feed it. For three days it cried and then one day it stopped crying. A little later the street was filled with the aroma of food. Several stopped with hopes of being part of the feast. Their eyes met something that could only happen in hell, a baby roasting over a fire. "Here, take a piece and eat it," cried a wild-eyed young woman. "He would have died anyway. If I live, I can have another child." Some took her up on the offer but Magdala became sickened and slowly walked away from the fire knowing that her own death was approaching.

Magdala lay down on the dirty pavement next to Chora. She had not stirred all day. It was if her body died before her soul left it. With hopes of death Magdala fell into a troubled sleep. She was awakened by someone jerking her hair and tying her hands and feet. She saw soldiers carrying Chora down the pavement. Dazed and in a semi-dream-like state, Magdala was not sure that any of this was happening. "Come on, all you varmints, get up, and walk over here. I wouldn't waste my time on you. But Titus thinks that you will bring a fair price on the market when you are fed. Come along here, get up, get up --get going"

Three days ago Titus had finally broken down the northern wall of the city of Jerusalem. Thousands of troops stormed the city expecting a vicious fight. Instead they found most of the people in the city lying dead in the streets. With a sickening horror the solders held their breath as they walked over the decaying bodies. Those that showed any life received a deadly blow from a sword. After only a few hundred feet into the city, Titus gave the order not to kill but to take captives. Magdala and Chora were taken captive.

Only a few healthy and strong souls took their stand against Titus. No one knows how these fighters survived. Some said that they had taken over the stores of grain in the temple for themselves. Within hours Titus had murdered all the rest of the revolutionaries that resisted him. Unknown to Titus, the leaders of the movement had escaped the night before and were taking refuge in a hideout in the desert. In a fit of anger, Titus gave the order, "Burn this God forsaken place." So the once majestic city that gleamed across the sky was razed to the ground. When the fire simmered low, Titus gave another order, "Knock down every stone, block, and board, leave nothing standing." The temple fell. And all those years, and thousands of workers, and millions of hours of work were gone, gone forever. It was as if the city never existed.

Magdala and Chora, with about another eleven thousand people, were being deported to Rome to be sold as slaves. Food came slowly but with it Magdala gained back some of her strength. As she sailed for Rome, Magdala grieved and missed Phoebe and John. She was ashamed of herself. Not once in the past three months had she thought of them, she only thought of surviving from one moment to the next. Some of the prisoners said that Rome had burned and pillaged towns in northern Judea too. Magdala wondered if her family was alive and if she would ever see them again.

As the ship sailed for Cyprus, it had to be put in for repairs at Attalia. In their haste to remove everyone from Judea, the Romans had put too many prisoners on board the ship. The ship would barely float. Oarsmen had to work over time to keep the vessel moving. One by one the captives walked toward the shore. "Come along, get over here, get down on the plank, will ya? Hey you're looking better aren't you little woman since you got some food in ya." Tied together like animals waiting for slaughter, the prisoners lined the streets of the city. The weather turned cold but no one offered them clothing or a blanket.

Magdala looked up into the eyes of a well-dressed young man who was inspecting each prisoner. Could he be a physician? a potential buyer? No one was allowed near the prisoners. Those were the captain's orders. His eyes passed up Magdala and then went on down the line and then turning back toward her he said, "Mother, mother, wake up. I have come to rescue you."Chora looked up and could hardly focus on the person who was shaking her. "Mother, it's Flavius, your son! Guard, release this woman." Standing firm the guard replied, "I cannot do that, Sir, I am under orders." Flavius pulled out a decree signed by Vespasian himself that released his mother and all her possessions.

"Guard, this is all a mistake. My mother should have never been taken prisoner. She is a citizen of Rome." As the guard untied the old woman, she murmured, "I must have my servant-girl go with me. I cannot live without her." Flavius was puzzled. He did not see any of their servants. "Mother, what are you talking about, your servant ...." and the old woman put her hand over his mouth. Grabbing Magdala by the arm she said, "Come with me girl, you are mine and no one else will have you."

Finally walking away from the guards, Flavius took them to a caravansarai outside of town. While they were changing into some clothes that Flavius had bought for them, Magdala began to cry, "I will never see Phoebe and John again. They are both dead, and I know it. What will I do? Where will I go? It would have been better off for me if I would have died in Jerusalem." The old woman felt her pain and reached out for her hand. She said ever so weakly and quietly, "Magdala, you have survived so much. Surely you must thank the Gods for your life. If your loved ones are alive, I know they will find you. You are really not far from the Judean coast and, perhaps, you will be able to travel home soon."

Flavius attempted to repay Magdala but she would not take the money. She only asked that he contact Rome and request that some of her inheritance be forwarded to her. "Please go to Ephesus with us," said Flavius. "My mother has told me the whole story. You would be welcome in our home for the rest of your life." Magdala was determined, "I must go back to Galilee. I have to find Phoebe and John, if they are alive." Flavius was very stern when he said, "Magdala, you can't go back now. It is much too dangerous. The fighting still continues in the north and south of what was Jerusalem. Rest here and when it is safe we will return with you. You must protect yourself, you are not well." And Magdala was not well. The old fevers had returned with an unpredictable violence.

Flavius arranged for an Asclepioi priest to help Magdala. Within an hour a woman knocked at her door. "Hello, I am the priestess you sent for, are you the one with the fevers?" The priestess looked at Magdala and marveled that she was still alive. "They call me Hygeia, I am here to help you."

CHAPTER FOURTEEN
THE ENDLESS SEARCH
C.E. 72

"There is power in the blood."

During the time in which Magdala lived, women found freedom only rarely. It is true, as in all lifetimes that money buys some freedom for some women, but never happiness or complete control over one's own life. Rome ruled with the fists of despotic steel. The state demanded worship of its own God, the Emperor. Death came to those who rejected this Divinity.

In a world where there is so little hope women could not worship a Divine male Emperor. He did bring occasional peace but the brutalities of the state overshadowed the fleeting security. There was no kindness or ecstasy in his reign. They needed to worship a God that aroused their passions. Their God would promise them power over their own lives. This God would kindle flames that would burst into an unspeakable union. That union would give them energy and sustain their empty, controlled, and servile lives.

Midwifed by fire and delivered by a blast of lightning, Dionysius, born of an illicit affair between Zeus and a human Semele, became a God who entered the soul of every kind of woman (rich and poor, slave and free) and sent them into the forests. There they witnessed a dynamic infusion of the Divine. In front of a throng of witnesses, there in the forests of Asia Minor Dionysius would meet his beloved Demeter. This clandestine assembly brought unspeakable rapture to the initiates who would awake the next morning knowing that they had become Gods themselves. Life could never be the same for they had tasted the power of the everlasting Divine.

Ignoring her own pain, Magdala could only think of her child. She imagined all sorts of dreadful things and was determined to find Phoebe and John. Rejecting the pleadings of Hygeia, Magdala traveled north and then east, toward the wars, toward Galilee, toward the unknown. The dilapidated old ox-cart reminded her of Philip and the day she escaped from the temple in Rome so long ago. She daydreamed often as she sat by Hygeia. The nights were very chilly as they crossed the mountains. Dressed like peasant farmers Magdala and Hygeia hoped to enter Judea unnoticed. All along their journey they questioned travelers that were fleeing north, "Have you seen a little girl, her name is Phoebe. She had long dark hair ...."

And the answer was always the same. There were thousands of children who lived on the streets of every city they passed. They had been abandoned or lost and Magdala could see Phoebe in every one of their faces. The war had uprooted so many in Judea that thousands of people began migrating to the outer edges of the Empire. Homeless, starving refugees populated every village they visited. Like lost souls they hovered around the small farming towns hoping to find work or food. Most of them ended up building little shanties or shacks to protect them from the cold and rain. Many kept on walking, hoping that they could outpace everyone else and find a place for themselves somewhere, somewhere!

Magdala had thanked Flavius and Chora for their generous offer of assistance. She declined to go with them to Ephesus but instead requested a loan, explaining that she had quite a lot of money in the Treasury in Rome. With them they took a signed and sealed letter from Magdala giving them the authority to extract part of her estate. Magdala and Chora reluctantly parted, like two relatives who had known each other all of their lives. Unknown to Magdala, Chora did not make it to Ephesus. On the way she died in her sleep. Flavius tore up the letter signed by Magdala and went on to become a celebrated Roman writer.

Magdala's journey toward the coastal cities of Judea proved to be an adventure beyond their wildest dreams. As Magdala and Hygeia roamed the countryside, following the Roman roads when possible, they camped one evening in a thick forest, high in the mountains, above the town of Lystra. There in the darkness, just before they retired for the evening, the two travelers witnessed a hideous ritual. Choosing not to light a fire because it was so late and they were so exhausted, they crawled under their wagon to rest. While sleeping, in the middle of the night, they were startled by shrieks and screams. Dancing sticks of fire trailed up the hill next to them. It looked like a long glowing snake. The process stopped only a few hundred feet away from them. They feared for their lives, but no one seemed to notice them.

Hushed chanting voices circled around the mountain stream. Clad in animal skins and little else, over twenty women began to sing songs and chant to Demeter, Goddess of the land. In the middle of the cheerfully dancing females was a young and beautiful male standing next to a blazing fire. His hands were bound and over his head hung a garment that prevented him from seeing the women.

Quietly Magdala and Hygeia edged closer to the clearing, peering through moss-covered vines. The circle began to sway faster while they chanted over and over again, "Great is Demeter, Give us Immortality." They were intoxicated and one by one the women would go to the man in the middle of the circle. Magdala and Hygeia could not see clearly what was happening when the women went into the circle. Only a few of the sticks had fire now. Hygeia explained, "I have heard that some worshippers of Demeter make love with the man whom they will sacrifice." Horrified, Magdala responded, "How can this be? Why would anyone want to kill an innocent man? "This ancient religion recognizes a female as ruler of the universe and in control of all sustenance. In order to fertilize and bring good things into this life, they believe that they must sacrifice someone. Women are too important, they are the ones who will bear the future generations. Men are expendable." Magdala cried, "Look what is happening now?

Both of the women feared for their lives but seemed incapable of saving the man. Hygeia warned, "If we enter their sacred space, they will sacrifice us too. We have no choice. We cannot win against twenty, young and armed females." The moments they stood in that hollow seemed like forever. They could see nothing now because the sticks with flames had gone out. The sounds of laughing, moaning, and rustling were very loud. Finally each woman returned to the fire in the middle of the circle and relit the stick they were carrying. They all sat down and began to eat something. "What is it, Hygeia?" "Magdala, do I need to tell you?" Magdala's throat felt like it was cut. Her stomach jerked as she heaved up everything she had eaten for dinner. The sky swirled and Magdala fell limp into the damp evening grass. The ghostly participants, faces bloodied, got up from their feast and began to sing and chant to their Goddess once again. They believed that they had devoured a meal with the Divine and would possess rebirth and eternal life.

For almost a week after Magdala witnessed the human sacrifice she remained deathly ill. The fevers kept coming stronger and stronger. Hygeia drove the wagon and attended to her the best that she could. The air was becoming more humid with each day they traveled toward Judea. Magdala complained of darkness and visions. She was dying and both of them knew it. Magdala had lived longer than any known patient who had contracted Fularia. The parasite was invading her brain and her heart.

Finally they reached the edge of Judea. Rome had relaxed some of its border patrols and people were allowed to travel the roads by day. They had no trouble on their way to Nazareth. As they rode down the scorched path, burned out villages and fields greeted them. The land had been stripped and no food was left for the people in the countryside or the villages. It was a pitiful sight. Many people going north would stop them and say, "Where are you going?" "To Capernaum," answered the hopeful travelers. "There is nothing left. Some city buildings remain but most everything else is gone. You won't recognize it. Come with us to the north. They say that there is food in Asia Minor." Magdala and Hygeia had little courage to tell them that there were thousands of people like them following a path that led nowhere.

Three days after crossing the border into Galilee, the women were within site of the city, bodies and rotting carcasses lay everywhere. They closed their eyes but knew that they had to keep searching. "There it is! Hygeia," cried Magdala as she pulled herself up in the wagon. "There is the house of the Zebedees." They climbed down off the wagon and as they walked they saw curtains flying through the open windows. The door was gone and so was all the furniture inside. Magdala stepped lightly into the old farmhouse to search for John and Phoebe. As her eyes adjusted to the light, a hoard of insects flew out at her. The only things left in the house were the fireplace and dirt floors. "Hygeia, they are all dead, I know it!"

Hygeia climbed to the roof of the old clay house. This is the place where they would eat after the sun went down. It looked out over a calm sea. A sea that did not remember the victims that lay on its beaches. Magdala had to drag herself out of the empty house. With no hope of ever finding or seeing Phoebe again, she thought she would go out to the barn where the family dried fish. It was there that Phoebe used to play beneath the rafters. As she moved the door slightly, she thought she saw something move. Her heart raced and she pushed harder to move the old wood door. "Phoebe, Phoebe, is that you? Hygeia, come here quickly."

The door was stubborn and Magdala needed Hygeia's help in order to open it. Inside she found nothings. In the old days, before the war, there might have been thousands of fishing hanging over smoldering coals. Now the smell was putrid and the walls were black. As they looked around the abandoned building, a board fell in the back of the barn. Magdala and Hygeia walked toward it. Suddenly a little boy jumped out from behind the board. His head was bleeding. Clutching a knife he screamed, "Get out of here! Leave me alone or I will kill you. " Magdala answered calmly, "Wait a minute. We won't harm you. We can help you. Hygeia is an Asclepioi priestess. Her medicine will heal your injury." The boy would not listen or perhaps did not understand, "Leave me alone or I will kill you," said the boy once again. Just as the words fell from his lips he melted into the floor.

The boy was so limp that neither of the two women could carry him. They wrapped him in one of their blankets and gently took care of his head. The board had fallen from the second story and hit him in the head while he was hiding. Half unconscious he drank a few sips of water. Hygeia was very concerned, "Magdala, we have to keep him awake. If he falls asleep he may never wake up again. His brain is swelling because of the injury." So for the next twenty-four hours both women took care of the little boy whom they did not know. By the next afternoon he was well enough to walk. "What do they call you," asked Magdala. The young boy responded, "I am Mark, son of Phanuel, servant to the Zebedees."

The little boy proceeded to tell them the gruesome story of how he had survived the war. The rest of the household was killed or taken as prisoners. Hiding in the storage cellar underneath the fish barn, he had survived on the vegetables that had been buried after the harvest. He did not know how long the Romans had been gone. Hygeia asked, "How long has it been since you have seen anyone?" Mark did not know. It could have been weeks.

Magdala was anxious to ask him about her daughter Phoebe and the Zebedee family. She hesitated and then looked him straight in the eyes, "Do you know what happened to Phoebe," "Oh, that little girl of John's?" asked Mark . "Yes," came the words from Magdala's trembling lips. "Oh, I used to play with her out in the fields. Some times we would go for a swim in the lake," answered Mark. "What happened to her? Was she killed or taken prisoner, asked Magdala again. "I don't know. I did not see it if it happened. The Zebedees left and took most of their furniture and valuables only days before the Romans invaded Capernaum. I heard mother Zebedee say that they were heading for a town in Asia. They thought they would be safe there. "Did they take Phoebe with them?" Mark answered, "I think so? She was very unhappy about leaving the farm. She kept calling for her mother."

Magdala began to cry, she was both relieved and afraid. She knew that her Phoebe could be alive. She had to continue her search. Who knows, her little girl could have been among the thousands of children on the road, camped and begging for food. It would take them a lifetime to find her. Hygeia knew that she had to help Magala. She put her arms around her and said, "Magdala, you must take care of yourself. Your little girl is strong and I am sure the family will do the best it can for her. You must sleep. Look at you, you have eaten very little in the past few days. Sleep for a while. We will have to head back toward Asia quickly. The cold weather is coming and we will not be able to travel through the mountains if it snows."

Magdala listened to her physician and fell asleep for almost two days. The hope of finding her daughter had kept her alive and now it had been briefly taken away from her. Within a couple of days Magdala and Hygeia were packed and ready to head north. Mark gave them some of the food that was still left in the cellar and they filled jugs with water from the Sea. "Mark will you go with us? You have nothing left here." And Mark reluctantly agreed to go with them, as they journeyed north in search of Phoebe and a better place for Magdala.

With the balmy wind of the Sea of Galilee behind them, they headed north through the mountains. Hygeia wanted to get Magdala to a house owned by a friend before the winter snows. Magdala was still determined to find her daughter. Each day they searched the roads they traversed and each day Magdala became weaker. The pain of the disease distorted her face, her eyes swelled, and she was unable to walk. Yet she kept going. It was her daughter that kept her alive.

Meanwhile John was worried about both Magdala and Phoebe. His ship had been detained at the port of Antioch in Syria by the Romans. He was suspected of selling food and stolen military equipment to the revolutionaries. Brought to court and kept in jail for months, he was finally found innocent. But the Romans wanted to watch him so they took him to Ephesus and placed him under house arrest. He was allowed to continue his fishing business but was not allowed to leave the city and had to be in his house at sundown every day.

In Ephesus, John accidently bumped into Flavius in the marketplace. Flavius told him of what he had seen of the war and then of a woman by the name of Magdala that had saved his mother's life during the siege of Jerusalem. Before the night was over John sent one of his servants on a ship bound for Attalia in search of both Magdala and Phoebe. Arriving only days after Magdala had left Capernaum, the servant discovered that she had gone north and but no one knew of her destination.

Magdala and Hygeia spent the winter searching for Phoebe. It was the same thing every day. As soon as they had eaten they would go one by one through the villages they passed through and knock on doors. They looked into the faces of hundreds and hundreds of starving and dying people. None had heard of the Zebedees but many said that they had seen little girls that resembled Phoebe. Over and over again Hygeia and Magdala would say, "Have you seen a little girl, about eight years old, who stand about his high, with dark brown hair, long hair, with small feet and hands and thin legs and arms?" Magdala in her delirium thought she had found her several times. She held out her arms to these starving and forgotten children but they did not have the strength or food to help them. Even if she gave all of her fortune to these children it would only sustain them for a week or so. The two became more and more frustrated as they journeyed toward Asia.

One happy and bright spot in their search was Mark. He became as concerned as they were in finding Phoebe. Magdala began to love this little boy who would play and encourage her. At night he slept with her. Magdala welcomed the warmth of another body close to her. Little Mark, like so many others in Magdala's life, became part of her family. She treated him like her son.

Mark had never experienced such love. Born into a slave's family, he had worked since he was old enough to walk. No one had ever paid any attention to him because he could not work like the other boys. One of his legs had been broken when he was very little and no one knew how to set it. It never healed properly. When he walked, he dragged it along the ground. This never stopped him; he had more enthusiasm for life than everyone around him.

Magdala's illness stabilized. Hygeia was constantly amazed at her endurance. No matter what obstacle was placed in her way, Magdala seemed to have the courage to find a way to go around it or conquer it. They searched the coast then headed toward the mountains of Bithynia. There high above the rocks was a cabin where they would stay. "If you do not take care of yourself you will die before you find Phoebe. Let's go to the mountains and rest. Perhaps we can hire someone to continue the search." Magdala protested, "Hygeia, Phoebe is life to me. She and John were all that I had in my life. I must find them. If I find Phoebe, I may find John. We have argued about this over and over, you know that I can not give up the search." Hygeia pleaded, "Please come with me to the mountains. Please take care of yourself." And so Magdala agreed. She had almost given up hope of finding John and Phoebe.

Unknown to Magdala, Hygeia, Mark, John or Phoebe was a hooded person who followed John everywhere in Ephesus. This mysterious stranger had pursued Magdala since the days she left the Great Temple in Rome. He had lost track of her during the sand storm in the desert when Magdala had been taken prisoner by the Herders. Stalking her like a hungry bear, Magdala would soon do battle with this monster.

Magdala and Hygeia soon traveled to Ephesus because of a note delivered from John through Flavius. Finding John in Ephesus hanging from a tree, Hygeia was assaulted by a man coming out of mob who broke her leg. Magdala searched for someone to help her but when she returned with help, Hygeia was gone. Out of nowhere a huge figure broke into the crowd and headed toward Magdala. Magdala felt her chest cave in. She tried to speak but blood oozed out of her mouth. Sinking to her knees, with both hands she pulled the knife out of her stomach. Wiping away the blood, she could see an emblem bearing the image of the golden sign of fire and then everything went black.

This ends our first in a series entitled *The Other Stories* that feature lives of ancient characters. Discover what happens to Demimonde while this series visits other ancient exotic places like Gibraltar, the shores of Mauretania Tingitana, and the land of the giants. If you are interested in being advised when the next volume is completed, please send your name and email address to selvidge@kc.rr.com

ABOUT THE AUTHOR

Marla J. Selvidge is currently director, professor, and founder of the Center for Religious Studies at the University of Central Missouri. The Center currently offers online programs in religious studies. Selvidge has authored or edited a dozen books including *Exploring the New Testament: Second Edition* (Prentice Hall, 2003) and *Notorious Voices: Feminist Biblical Interpretation, 1550–1920* (Paragon House, 1996). She will soon write a book about why people love Elvis while exploring his life-long love affair with religions. Selvidge earned her PhD from Saint Louis University. She resides in Missouri with her companion and husband, Thomas C. Hemling, a PhD chemist and vice president of an animal health company.